THE
Little
Brothers

Other books by Dorothy Salisbury Davis

Crime Fiction
SHOCK WAVE
WHERE THE DARK STREETS GO
THE PALE BETRAYER
BLACK SHEEP, WHITE LAMB
OLD SINNERS NEVER DIE
A GENTLEMAN CALLED
DEATH OF AN OLD SINNER
A TOWN OF MASKS
A GENTLE MURDERER
THE CLAY HAND
THE JUDAS CAT

Novels
GOD SPEED THE NIGHT (with Jerome Ross)
ENEMY AND BROTHER
THE EVENING OF THE GOOD SAMARITAN
MEN OF NO PROPERTY

THE
Little
Brothers

Dorothy Salisbury Davis

Charles Scribner's Sons   *New York*

1 3 5 7 9 11 13 15 17 19 c/c 20 18 16 14 12 10 8 6 4 2

Printed in the United States of America
Library of Congress Catalog Card Number 72-11134
SBN 684-13397-0 (cloth)

THE
Little
Brothers

1 The Little Brothers were ruled by a code. Not only did they try to live by it themselves, they tried to make others live by it as well. It was based on pride and purity, and its purpose was to protect their own. It was made up out of the folklore of Sicily and the imagination of the members. The club was the most exclusive in a neighborhood where virtually every male, man or boy, belonged to a club of some sort. The Little Brothers' rites were secret and their works charitable and patriotic. Most families were proud to say that a son of the house was a Little Brother.

Candidates were nominated by members, selected by lot, and then only when a circumstance in the community provided what was called "the ordeal" by which a boy could prove his worthiness. There were never more than twenty active members at a time, and so far no one who had outgrown the club was known to have violated its oath of lifetime secrecy.

Angie Palermo was not even sure he wanted to be a Little Brother. At sixteen, he was a loner, a dreamer. His mother kept pushing him from her and pulling him to her. Most of the time he hated her. He hated Mr. Rotelli, her boyfriend, even more. Angie had a friend he also hated, mostly because he was afraid of him, and when "Fat Ric" said he was putting Angie up for the Little Brothers, Angie was afraid to say he didn't want to be one. Since his name was not likely to come up for some time, Angie tried to forget about it although once in a while he fantasied himself a leader among the Little Brothers, who took an honored part that year in the organization of Italian American Day.

It was a hot summer in New York, and Mr. Rotelli was around the house most of the time. Angie found a rooftop hideout for himself. He found it because of a girl he thought the most beautiful person he had ever seen: she was blond and tall and graceful, not at all like the girls he knew. He sometimes watched for her to go into Allioto's Delicatessen on Hester Street, and then followed her home, keeping at a distance so that she would not see him. Having grown up on the streets of Little Italy, he knew many hiding places. He knew the tenements well enough to try the trap door to the roof opposite the building where she lived. It gave him no trouble and, after he had gone up there a few times, he got into the habit of pulling the fire ladder up after him. Gradually he provisioned himself—several tins of anchovies, olives, peanuts, a couple of books; he devised a makeshift tent which he sometimes pretended was a boat on a shimmering sea, and in the heat the tarpaper often bubbled up like black water. Sometimes he saw the girl when she came to the window and tended the plants she kept on the fire escape. She lived on the top floor.

Angie was a watcher: of stars, of birds, of planes, of people. He liked people as long as they didn't try to smother him. And yet he wanted to be smothered. Sometimes. He liked it that people liked him: he knew it was so because he had overheard an old woman of the neighborhood say he was the nicest boy on Elizabeth Street.

He was a watcher, which made "the ordeal," when it was explained to him, seem more romantic than anything he had supposed could come of initiation into the Little Brothers.

Ric had left a phone message with his mother, and to make sure Angie found out he was wanted by the Little Brothers at eight o'clock that night, Ric also left word with Mrs. Niccoli who sat on a chair outside his building most of the day and well into the night.

Angie needed all his courage to walk into the basement clubroom where the five members of the council waited at the round poker table. The boys did not play poker. They had salvaged the table because there was a gash in it. Ric introduced him which wasn't necessary. Angie knew them all and they knew him, Tony from school, the others from around the neighborhood: Pete the Turk, a wiry youngster so-called because of his round head; Gabby from Gabriel, not because he talked so much; Ric; and Big Louis, their captain and the oldest. He was scheduled to go to college in the fall. Ric wanted to be made captain when Louis left. He had told that to Angie; he told everything to Angie and made him listen. He didn't make Big Louis listen. He started to say something and Louis said, "Shut up, Bonelli."

Angie was required to take a blood oath of secrecy. He was given a small sharp knife with which to draw blood from his own thumb. When he managed on the third jab, each of the council drew his own blood in turn. Angie muttered the words "blood bank," in his nervousness needing to make a joke and afraid to make it. If anyone heard there was no sign. Louis squeezed a drop of blood in a saucer, and motioned Angie to do the same. The others followed in the order Louis named them. Ric was last, and it crossed Angie's mind that Ric wasn't ever going to be their captain. That thought reassured him until he realized that Ric's being the last made a symbolic circle which closed Angie in.

Louis recited the credo of the Little Brothers as solemnly as he sometimes read the lector's prayers at Mass. It concerned service to God, family, community, and country, loyalty to one another, and obedience to the code. Angie had pretty well known these precepts from Ric, and he would have guessed that the Little Brothers disapproved of drunkenness and drugs. A notable omission was reference to sex, except that he supposed it was covered in the "protection of one another's sisters."

Angie swore another oath, this one of loyalty. Ric took away the saucer and washed it with spit and kleenex.

The folding chair creaked under Louis as he leaned back and took his wallet from his pocket. He was a big, broad-shoul-dered youth. He became comradely with Angie as he took a newspaper clipping from the wallet and gave it to the novice to read. Four lines in length, it did not have a heading:

> Wong Lee, proprietor of the Yellow Chrysanthemum on Mott Street, died of suffocation last night when a fishbone lodged in his windpipe while he was eating dinner at his own restaurant.

Louis said, "You know who he was, don't you?"

"I heard of him. He owned a building where somebody I know used to live."

"A slumlord."

"It was two or three years ago," Angie said. All he could remember was his mother saying that the Chinaman had it coming to him.

"I put the Killing Eye on him a week before it happened."

Angie didn't say anything. The Brothers had him fixed with their eyes. He felt like a roach on a pin. Louis and the others waited in silence for him to gather the implications for himself. He tried to keep his fingers from trembling as he gave the clipping back.

"It hasn't worked as strong for all the Brothers," Louis said, "but something pretty awful's happened to everybody a Brother put the Eye on."

More silence until Angie asked, "How does it work?"

"You'll find out while you're doing it."

"To just anybody?"

Louis shot a glance at Ric that blamed him for Angie's stupidity. "You wouldn't be here, Angie, if we didn't have a candidate that deserves the Killing Eye. Do you know the religious articles shop on Hester Street?"

"Next to Allioto's deli?" Louis nodded. Angie had seen the girl he so admired stop there a couple of times on her way to or from the delicatessen. He had wondered why, but he had not given it much thought. She never stayed very long.

"It's run by a Jew named Grossman. He's your target."

"But you got to tell me what he's done," Angie said.

"No. You're going to tell us when it's over. Then we'll know

4

if you're really one of us. You got a week, midnight tonight till midnight. You'll scout the place and watch him. Who knows, maybe you'll find a way to scare him to death yourself. You'll wish him dead, and take a Little Brother's word for it, when you get to know him, you'll mean it. Pick a weapon. Concentrate. You got imagination. But just remember: you're on your own and you're sworn to secrecy. Under pain . . . of what?"

"The Killing Eye."

"On you," Louis added. It wasn't necessary.

Angie walked in a daze for a little while after he left the clubroom, his thoughts tripping over one another. He had not had a chance to say whether or not he wanted to take those oaths. It was taken for granted that everyone wanted to be a Little Brother. Pick a weapon: he was going to have to pretend he was after someone he knew, just to get the whole thing going. Fat Ric came to mind at once. At the moment, he couldn't even remember what Mr. Grossman looked like. He put his thumb with the cut to his mouth, sucked it and spat. He decided that he should have a knife. He had always wanted a hunting knife. He had enough money saved and he decided to buy one the next day. Then he walked to Hester Street.

As soon as he saw the shop he realized that he knew more about its proprietor than he had thought. The window was clouded with dust. So were the many-colored statuettes of saints on display. Off to the corner was a collection of long-faced saints, icons. There was a Ukrainian Orthodox church on the corner. It seemed queer that a Jew would run such a shop in Little Italy. He remembered having seen the old man come out one night and lock the door. He'd had to open it again to let the cat out. The cat shot past its master, and then, a minute later, darted past him again, as Mr. Grossman went up the stairs between his shop and the delicatessen.

There was not much light in the shop, but there was some. Angie could not see Mr. Grossman, but a tall, heavy-shouldered black man stood at the counter, his back to the door. There was a little motion to his arms which Angie tried to figure out: he decided the man might be counting out money. The black man cocked his head and before he could turn Angie moved along the street. It was almost dark. The street lights had come on. Angie went to the end of the block, crossed the street, and came back on the other side. He could hear the kids playing on the side streets, but Hester Street was almost deserted. He wished there were more people. He ducked down behind a parked car. From overhead came the whispery flutter of the red, white, and green pennants strung across the street. Through the pennants, he could see a woman walking back and forth with a baby in her arms on the third floor over Grossman's.

The black man came out of the shop carrying a package the size of a shoebox. He walked swiftly down the street to the vacant lot where the boys sometimes played stickball against the side of the building. A car door slammed, a motor revved up, and a shiny black car shot out over the curb, the wheels screaming as it turned and sped toward the Bowery.

Angie returned to the shop window. Grossman was making a small oblong packet out of newspaper around which he put a rubber band. The boy was sure it was money. The cat was watching, sitting on the counter. It put a paw to the package and the old man gave it a swat that knocked it off the counter. When Grossman sat down at a desk at the back, only the back of his head in sight, Angie went away. He felt a shiver down his back. It was not yet midnight. He did not have to start thinking about the Killing Eye till then, but he already hated Grossman for the way he treated the cat.

During the week that followed, Angie collected several observations that confirmed the evil of Ben Grossman. He saw a policeman getting a pay-off in a white envelope into which Angie had seen Grossman putting money. The old man didn't sell a single statue in the times when Angie was watching. Once he dusted the saints in the window, most of whom Angie had by then identified, St. Anthony, St. Francis, The Little Flower, several Virgin Marys. Dusting one of them, Grossman

6

had spat on her. On the third day, Angie grew bold enough to make his presence known to the shopkeeper. He brought an old sock from home and wiped a six-inch square in the dirty window at his own eye level. From then on he periodically stared in at the old man through the clean place. It could not have been the first time Grossman was annoyed by the youth of the neighborhood: most of the time he ignored Angie ·although he muttered a lot to himself. Once in a while he shook his fist at the boy. Otherwise, he kept his eyes on the newspaper which was always spread out before him on the counter. He sat on a high, backless stool.

Angie explored the hallway where Grossman went up and down to his second-floor apartment or to the hall bathroom. Grossman did not bother to lock the shop when he went up on short excursions. Only once did Angie see the woman outside the third-floor apartment: there was apparently only the one toilet in the building. Her husband, a tall dark-browed Sicilian, did the shopping when he came home from work. Angie drew swastikas along the hallway walls with colored markers. He was not sure what they meant, only that it was the worst thing you could do to a Jew. Nor was his artwork very good. He had a hard time getting the correct angles on the symbol. Maybe once or twice a day, somebody would go into the shop and buy a religious medal or a holy picture—never a painted expensive one. Otherwise, there was nobody except the old man and his cat, until the evening the black man came again.

Angie was sitting in the entryway to the leather goods factory across the street. The factory was closed for the month of August. When the black man went in the shop Angie gave him a minute and then crossed the street and looked in through his clean spot in the glass. Grossman poked his head around. He saw Angie and said something. The black man whirled around: Angie saw only the beginning of the move-ment. He skittered along to the hallway and hid himself behind the door which always stood open. But the black man came and pulled Angie out from behind the door. He lifted him from the floor like Grossman might his cat. He had a gold

7

tooth and a scar on his upper lip. He said into Angie's face: "Little fascist kid, you want your throat cut?"

Angie, with a knife sheathed in his own belt, said "No."

"Then get out of here and don't ever come back. Hear?"

He hurled Angie into the street, the boy kicking to get his feet on the ground. As soon as he got them under him, he ran and kept running. But he circled the block as far as the far side of the lot which he had reconnoitered after the first time he had seen the black man. He waited in the shadow of the building, safe on the other side of a high cyclone fence, and watched the black limousine until the man came, again carrying a package. Again he drove off in a fury of noise and dust. Angie felt sure there was one of the statues in the package, and he figured that inside the statue there had to be horse. Heroin.

Angie could not watch Grossman night and day, but it was safe to say he thought about him most of the time. He wished him many deaths, but he wished him dead most fiercely for the way he treated his cat, giving it food one minute, kicking it, whacking it the next. The one good thing that happened to Angie owing to "the ordeal" was that not once during the week had Ric Bonelli come near him, not at home or on the street.

On the last day, Angie did not get to Grossman's until late. There was word about that a film company shooting on location on Grand Street was hiring people for a crowd scene. Angie was hired. His was one of the faces in a group of people who were supposed to be watching a plane when it exploded in the sky. More than most things, he wanted to be an actor. His face ached when he got through from screwing it up in horror. He hoped the director would "discover" him, but an assistant paid him ten dollars and had him sign a release. When he was leaving, he saw the girl who lived opposite his hideout. She got out of a station-wagon in costume. She was an actress. Angie would have postponed his watch of Grossman a little longer, except that she went into a warehouse for "interior shooting." But seeing her weakened his concentration on Mr. Grossman. For the rest of the day he kept fantasying himself playing her lover. He wished to God he would grow a little taller, suddenly, miraculously. His mother had assured him he was all through growing at fifteen but he had managed another inch in the last year in spite of her. The evening dragged on until finally at eleven he took up his place at the shop window. It was crazy that Grossman should still be open at that hour, but he always was. He sat at the counter, his sour, crinkled face in his hands, his elbows on the newspaper.

The cat jumped up on the counter, giving the old man a start. Grossman folded his arms and looked at it. Angie wanted it to run; he could hear the abuse in the old man's voice while the cat, poor cat, was hoping for the purrs of love. Angie bit his lip and closed his eyes. It did no good. In his mind's eye he saw first the stroke and then the clout for which the cat never seemed to be prepared. He heard its yowl and felt its pain and surprise and rage and helplessness. He knew the feelings in his bones.

When Angie opened his eyes, the old man was staring back at him. He came from behind the counter, climbed up among the religious articles, and kicked those in his way from beneath his feet. Angie was fascinated, held rooted as by a mesmerist, for Grossman himself never took his eyes from the place in the window where Angie's face showed through. The nearer he came, the more terrible his eyes seemed to the boy, bits of color in them like fire in coals. Angie felt the curse turned back on him. He put up his arm and blocked out the eyes. Only then was he able to break away and run. He ran all the way to his hideout. It was not until he had pulled the ladder up behind him and closed the trap door that he felt safe from an unnamable evil. He knew that no matter what happened to him with the Little Brothers, he would never go near Mr. Grossman's again. Even Ric could not make him do that. He took the knife from his belt and buried it, sheath and all, in the sand bucket he had stolen from the floor below. At the time he took the bucket, he had thought of using it in an emergency as a cat uses sand. Was Mr. Grossman himself on drugs? That possibility soothed him. It was a kind of explanation.

He went to the parapet and looked at the windows across the way. He promised himself that he would go home soon; he would wait a little while and see if the girl's lights came on . . . Mr. Rotelli would be waiting with Angie's mother, and if there was an argument, he would take Angie's side, which Angie hated. He looked at the street below. In the longest time only one car passed, and four men, one of them staggering from one side of the walk to the other, then back, as though he was aboard ship on a stormy sea. If the girl came now with someone chasing her . . . How often he had imagined himself leaping down fire escape to fire escape to save her. He had never seen an Italian as blond as she was; his mother said there were blue-eyed Italians, mostly from Firenze. He wished his family had come from there instead of Sicily.

Sicilian bitch. He thought of the night he heard his father call his mother that. Then he'd gone roaring out of the house, slamming one door after another like a string of firecrackers. Angie, in bed, had stopped his ears, trying not to hear his mother's wails. He had not yet fallen asleep when she came into his room hours later, but he pretended that he was. He moved away from her touch as though in his sleep. But she had knelt by the bed and stroked him, taking down the sheet. That was in August, too. And to this August, three years later, he could feel her warm wet lips on his behind. In the morning when she'd found his bed was wet, she had beaten him with the yardstick. Sicilian bitch.

The light flashed on in the girl's apartment. She opened the window wide and pulled the shade three-quarters down. It wouldn't go any further, Angie knew, and this time as soon as she turned her back it flew up again, all the way to the top. She couldn't reach it. A man came up behind her and drew it down as far as it would go. A minute later he put a chair with its back to the window, and hung his coat over it, leaving but two tiny squares of light on either side.

The lump in Angie's throat was hard to swallow. It did not help to ask himself what he expected—that she was some kind of Immaculata? Who was? And who was Angelo Palermo to her? What hurt the most, he persuaded himself, was being shut out that way: it was like a door in the face. He eased himself out of grief by guessing at who the tall man might be. A movie star? He seemed older. She would have to be with an older man, not some kid who had played an extra. A writer maybe. Or a choreographer. It was a word Angie loved. He sometimes dreamed that he was a dancer. Alone, he danced at home, moving the furniture out of the way. So he made up in his mind a picture of the man and the girl whose name he did not know: they came up to the roof overhead from her apartment to look at the stars or the New York skyline, and then they discovered the dancing boy. Angie took off his dark tee shirt and, naked to the waist, began to dance. He leaped and twisted and made shapes with his arms, wings of his hands, arrows of his feet. What I need, he thought and laughed aloud at his own wit, is a fiddler on the roof.

The light went out in her apartment and the coat still hung on the back of the chair. The music inside Angie stopped. After a while he put on his shirt and wished he had a sweater also. The sea-scented dampness seeped into him, and the longing. He watched the lights of a plane and thought of his father in California, his mother, and the wedding ring she couldn't get off her finger though in bursts of anger she pulled at it until her finger was raw. He thought of the diamond ring Mr. Rotelli wore and his polished fingernails. He thought of Mr. Grossman going up to his apartment on the second floor, and how the cat darted past him on the stairs. Sometimes the old man would sit down on the stoop and take off his shoes and the cat would go round them, bobbing its head to and from them as much as to say how they stank. Angie thought of his father again and the laced shoes that supported his ankles. His mother worked at the bakery ovens now where he had worked before he went away. When she got up at a quarter to five, she would know that Angie had not come home. He ought to go home, but he didn't want to. He tried to fall asleep in his tent, but he couldn't. Just as he was dozing off, he woke up in a turmoil of fears. Which made him angry. Why should he be afraid of his mother, for example? Or of Mr. Grossman, for that matter? He got up and went to the building's edge again. The coat was still blocking the window; they'd have her fan alongside the bed. Now he knew what pain was, a new kind of pain that almost felt good because it made him want to fight. The man was probably a lot stronger than Fat Ric, of whom he was afraid, and yet Angie knew he could fight the man till death.

He began to study the fire escape where all the plants were and how steps went up from it with two graceful rails wheeling onto the roof.

2 The vestibule door to her building stood open. The apartment doors would be locked and double bolted. Angie glided noiselessly up one flight of stairs, then another. Here the fire steps to the roof were on springs. They hugged the ceiling. Angie leaped and brought them down with a shower of dirt and rust. He went up, lithe as a cat and shouldered open the roof door. He stepped out into the open.

He had never felt so keyed up at the prospect of mischief which could get him into serious trouble. He truly did not care. It was almost as though he wanted that to happen. He went over the edge of the roof and down the iron steps backwards. He looked down only once, to make sure where the flower pots were. He kept thinking of himself as a cat, a soft-footed, sure-footed cat. He squatted outside the window, listening. The only sound from within was the whirr of the fan. His nerves tingled at the thought of a sudden explosion in there, the man leaping up, the girl screaming. But the only other sounds were far away, the rumble of Con Ed, the wet, hissing sound of tires on the Bowery, the squeal and groan of subway cars climbing out of the ground onto the Williamsburg Bridge. He put his hand to the coat: it was as soft as belly fur. Slowly, slowly, he drew it from the chairback into his arms. He felt a wallet in the inside pocket, took it out and left it on the chair, a chivalrous act that satisfied him even more with himself. No one awoke. The whole city might well have been asleep. With the collar of the jacket between his teeth, he climbed back up, and once on the roof, put the jacket on. It was soft, warm, expensive, and except for the sleeves which were too long, it fit him well. He had missed an envelope in the pocket from which he had taken the wallet. Which was all right. A letter would tell him to whom and where if he someday wanted to make restitution. There was a small flat key in the change pocket which he resolved not to think about.

He dropped from the roof to the floor below and left the attic door open. They could use some air in that hall. He went down the stairs with dancer's feet, but the minute he reached the street he was a kid scared of the dark again, and even more scared of its patches of light and the shadows within them. Heaps of rubbish looked like crouched bodies. A man at the wheel of a parked car was asleep or stoned or stone dead. He could not go home with the coat, and suddenly he was afraid to return with it to his hideout. He wanted people, lots of people and lights everywhere. He kept to the middle of the street and half-walked, half-ran to Houston Street.

There the street lights hung in neon spans and cars passed regularly in both directions. Bowery bums sprawled in doorways of old clothes shops and hardware stores, drunken men who stank of their own juices, but harmless, not like junkies. Across the street was dangerous, the beat of the blacks and Puerto Ricans, and the iron-faced motorcycle crowd. It was no-man's-land to the Little Brothers. Angie clung to his own side. He wanted to get to the West Village, and the closer he came to it, the safer he felt. He wanted to see himself wearing the coat. The glimpses he caught in store windows tantalized him. Near Lafayette Street, he passed a restaurant where the whole counter wall was a mirror. Angie went back. Two men sat on stools near the back and a waitress was pouring coffee for them. He turned under the cuffs of the jacket and made sure he had his wallet in his hip pocket. He went in and sat near the door.

He ordered coffee, hardly taking his eyes from himself in the mirror. The coat was a pearly gray and over his dark blue tee shirt, it looked perfect on him. His chin was darker than the rest of his face: some day he was going to have a beard as heavy as his father's. His black hair was long, but not in the hippy way. He looked moody, like a musician or an artist, especially when he scowled and stared into his own wide dark eyes. He looked older than sixteen. The waitress said "Thank you, sir" for the quarter tip he gave her. He sipped the coffee black although he wanted sugar and cream in it. He was afraid the cuff would come out if he stretched his hand for the bowl and pitcher.

He grew bold with the bitter heat in his stomach and took the envelope from the inside pocket. It wasn't a letter: it was an American Airlines folder with a plane ticket inside for a return flight to Los Angeles; he was a minute or two figuring that out. The passenger's name was Phillips. Angie thought at once of his father. What would he say if his youngest son showed up . . . ?

The waitress pushed a damp cloth between his cup and the sugar bowl. "Going somewhere?"

He looked up at her. She was a plump girl with big breasts and tired eyes that made her look older than she probably was. Her hair was a shade of red he'd never seen before. "Los Angeles," he said in his deepest voice, and thought that maybe it might be so.

She jerked her head toward the men down the counter. "They're going to Cincinnati tonight."

Angie glanced at them. They wore field jackets. "Truck drivers?"

"Long distance movers. That's why this dump stays open at night. We're between the bridge and the tunnel."

Angie couldn't think of anything to say. He kept trying to look up at her face, but her breasts were eye level to him. Finally he looked at his nose in the coffee mug.

"Know where I'm going tomorrow?" she said without enthusiasm. "Palisades Amusement Park."

"That's nice," Angie said. He had never been there. He put the mug down carefully in the circle it had already made on the counter.

"What's so nice? I got to pay my own way."

"You wouldn't if I was taking you," Angie said. He wanted to say something nice to her. He could see the dark nipples through the uniform.

"So ask me my objections?"

He made himself look up. She darted the tip of her tongue out at him. She wasn't pretty, but she wasn't ugly either. Little lights had come into her eyes.

Angie pulled a sad face and put the envelope back in his pocket where he patted it. "I wish I could," he mumbled. One cuff was coming out of its fold. He put his hands beneath the counter and tried with his fingernails to make a crease that would hold.

She shrugged as much as to say she hadn't expected it to turn out any better. "Do you live in California?"

"Not yet," he said, afraid to lie about a place he knew nothing about.

"I didn't think so. Not enough sunshine vitamin C." She reached for the coffee maker and refilled his cup.

"I'm going to work in a movie. My father's out there. He sent for me."

"Is he a big shot or something?"

Angie said, "I guess so."

"What's your name in case you turn out to be a real Dustin Hoffman."

Angie grinned. "He's my favorite actor too."

"You know what?" she said, cocking her head to one side. "You got a nicer smile than him. I mean it."

Angie thought of the nine dollars minus forty cents in his pocket. "If I was to get delayed, I mean—you know—I'd take you to Coney Island tomorrow."

"I'd rather go to Palisades. It's a nicer class of people."

"I like the ocean," Angie said. He knew the price of a subway token. Two bus fares were something else.

"It's got a swimming pool with real waves," she said.

"I couldn't go anyway," Angie said. "I got this reservation."

"Then what did you ask me for?"

"Wishing," he said.

"Wishin', pishin'," she said, and almost broke the coffee jug when she slammed it back on the burner.

One of the truckers signaled for his check. There was a lot of laughing as she toted up the figures. Angie studied himself in the mirror. It stood to reason that he looked older or she wouldn't have made insinuations. When the men walked out one of them winked at Angie and stuck his tongue in his cheek. Angie was pretty sure what it meant.

The girl rang up the money in a noisy cash register. "I'm going to close up now," she said.

"Okay."

"You don't have to go till I'm ready." He could not quite see what she was doing at the register, but when she turned away from it she left the drawer open. It looked empty. Wherever the money was, nobody was going to break into an open cash register. She took the dishes out of the washer and stacked them on the backboard, glancing now and then at Angie in the mirror.

The clock on the back wall showed twenty past three. A night could be a very long time. He could still make it home and into bed and even asleep before his mother got up for work. If he could sleep, which he doubted.

"Why don't you talk to me, big shot? What kind of a movie are you going to be in?"

"I'm not."

"That's what I figured. You worked as an extra today on *Grand Street*, right?"

He nodded.

"I had a flock of them in here tonight when they quit work at eleven." She brought the coffee maker. "I'm only going to throw it out." She was about to pour some in Angie's mug.

"No, thanks. It makes me . . ."

"Be my guest." She made an open-handed gesture toward the washroom door.

"Maybe I better," Angie said. He stood up and tried to walk at his best height. He would look funny from behind, the expensive sports jacket over jeans and sneakers. Everything was so quiet. In the washroom he tried not to make any noise urinating. The water flushed like a busted hydrant. He looked at himself in the tarnished mirror: all eyes and no jaw. He threw his head up, his shoulders back.

When he went out Fat Ric was sitting at the counter.

Ric had on his old black sweater and the way he was hunched up, he looked swollen inside it. Even his eyes were puffy. Something had happened to him in the week since Angie had seen him. Angie didn't care about that. He wasn't even curious. But he did care about how easy it had been for Ric to find him and start messing in his life again as soon as "the ordeal" was finished.

Ric didn't bat an eye as Angie approached. Angie thought of trying to march past him and right out the door, but he could feel Ric's eyes marking his every step.

"Congratulations," Ric said when Angie got close to him. It sounded sarcastic.

"Huh?"

"Didn't you know? The Jew just choked to death on a matzo ball." Ric's shoulders shook at his own joke. The sound wasn't funny and his face hardly showed the laugh at all.

Angie felt a little sick.

"What about a Jew?" the waitress said, an edge to her voice. She was watching them both in the mirror, her lipstick poised in her hand.

"Nothing personal," Ric said. "Come on, baby, a cup of coffee. Instant's okay. I want to tell Angie something."

"Too bad, but you got the wrong shop." She proceeded with the lipstick, but her eyes met Angie's in the mirror. There was something protective in them: he caught it. God knows what she had caught from his.

"Sit down," Ric said to Angie. He kicked his foot out at the stool next to his. Angie climbed up on it. He kept holding the cuffs in place, his hands in his lap. Ric did not seem to notice.

"I got a feeling it's going to work for you, Angie."

Angie knew what he meant, but he said, "What?"

"Are you kidding, Little Brother?"

18

"I don't know," Angie said, meaning he did not know whether the Killing Eye would work on Grossman or not. He had the feeling Ric knew what had happened at the window. "How come you're . . ." He couldn't even finish what he started to say.

"Just happened to come this way tonight. Some day I'm going to get me a job that ain't pushing stiffs around at four in the morning." That was Ric's one big joke, and he said it loud enough for the girl to hear. He loaded sides of beef on butcher's row, West Fourteenth Street. "I work in a cow morgue."

"Very funny," the waitress said.

"I never seen that coat before, Angie." Ric leaned back to take a better look.

"It's mohair," Angie said. He did not know what it was.

"I was wanting to see you tonight," Ric said, "but I didn't want to get in the way of you know what. I wanted to tell you about me and Pa."

Angie didn't want ever to hear about Ric and his father again. His father was a kind of cripple. He didn't go on crutches, but he couldn't work and he fought all the time with Ric, and Ric took it out on Angie.

"I almost killed him tonight. He's in the Bellevue Hospital."

Angie didn't say anything. He wasn't even sure he believed it.

But the waitress said, "No kidding?"

"No kidding, baby. So how about the java?"

"Okay, Angie?"

He was surprised she'd asked him. "I guess so."

Ric said: "You two pals or something? Introduce me, Angie."

Angie could think of only one name, Alice. "Alice, this is Ric Bonelli."

Alice gave him the briefest of nods. She turned the burner on under the coffee maker. "What happened to your father?"

"He hates my guts, but he lives off me just the same. I got a brother a lawyer and a sister married practically to a bank. I got to go to bed early you know to get some sleep and right in the middle of the night he wakes me up to go out and get him a bottle of wine. I said I wasn't going, and he was griping about being cooped up, and the first thing I knew he's broke a window and he's shouting about being free, America the land of the free, stuff like that. Which I don't take making fun of, as you know, Angie. So I got kind of rough with him. Then old lady Niccoli next door starts pounding on the wall. By then I was getting crazy mad and I knowed I had to get out of there or smash him or something. I was going to go to your place, Angie. Then I remembered. I just went out and walked and . . ."

"In your nightclothes?" Alice interrupted.

"I'd fell asleep with my clothes on," Ric said. "Anyway, I got him his stinking wine and went back, and what do you think he did? He started in on me all over again."

Angie had never seen Ric quite this way before although he had heard variations of the story, the fights, the wine; even Mrs. Niccoli ran through Ric's life story like a witch, sticking her nose in all the time.

"Slow down," Alice said. "If I'm going to make you coffee I want to hear what happened."

"I got him the wrong kind of wine or something. I was trying to calm him down so I poured some in a glass for myself. He's always wanting me to take a drink with him. 'Okay, Pa,' I says to him, 'give a toast.' " Ric wiped his nose on the sleeve of the sweater.

"So what did you toast to?" Alice asked.

"Life. You don't drink a toast to death."

"I myself drink to people," Alice said and dumped a spoonful of instant coffee into a mug. "Angie?"

"No thanks."

"I know. You'd have to pee. Go on, Mr. Bonelli."

"How come you call me that?"

"It's your name, isn't it?"

"Yeah, yeah, only I don't think of it as me. I think of my old man. What if he dies, Angie?"

"Wasn't it an accident, whatever happened?"

"In here it was no accident." Ric thumped on his chest.

Alice poured the water and shoved the steaming mug across the counter. "What did you do, hit him over the head with the bottle?"

"That's very funny, lady, because it's exactly what I did. I got even madder, see, when the old dame next door kept pounding on the wall. So I went out in the hall. I was going to let her have it. I mean who the hell is she? She lives alone and tries to live our lives for us, see. She'd have me in a penitentiary if she could. She wrote Fuck in the hall once and blamed it onto me. I know. She left off the 'k' like in Ric the way I spell it. Where was I?"

"Getting fucked by the old lady," Alice said, without cracking a smile.

Angie flinched in spite of himself. He'd heard it often enough, but it didn't sound right coming from any woman.

"You got some sense of humor," Ric said. "The old man was trying to hold me back . . ."

"Drink your coffee," the waitress said. "It ain't such a great story. It happens all the time in the Bronx."

"Boy, you're some wisecracker, aren't you?" Ric said. He pulled at Angie's arm. Angie had to turn his way even though Ric's sweater stank and he was trying not to smell it. "When I swung at him, you know that railing running along the stairs? He crashed through it all the way down the stairs on his head. Niccoli started to scream. She woke up the whole fucking building, and I was still trying to get the old man to come to when the cops broke in."

"Why didn't they arrest you?" Alice asked.

Ric looked at her as though she was completely stupid. "He ain't dead yet." He took one sip of the coffee and set the mug down, spilling it. He pushed it away. "This stuff is poison. Come on, Angie. I'll buy you a decent cup somewheres."

"I can't, Ric . . ." He looked at the waitress who looked like she was going to throw the coffee in Ric's face. "I promised to take Alice home after she closed up."

She threw the coffee into the sink, wiped out the mug with a paper napkin, and put it back on the shelf,

Angie remembered then that she mentioned the Bronx.

Ric said, "No you don't. No chick's going to come between one Little Brother and another."

Alice said, "Fat Boy, there ain't a chick alive who'd want to come between you and anything. Now, vacate or I'm going to take a fork to you and let some of the grease out—a guy who'd hit his own father."

"Say Fat Boy to me again, baby, and I'll take this place apart for you."

"Fat Boy."

Ric mumbled about it being enough to wreck one place in a night and slid off the stool carefully—like he had a sore behind. He pulled his sweater down and then again wiped his nose on his sleeve. "I'm getting a cold or something."

Alice went to the door pulling the cord to one fluorescent light after the other.

Angie tried to get past Ric but the fat one caught him and put an arm across his shoulders so that they walked in the blue gloom together. "What if he dies, Angie?"

Angie did not believe it. At least he did not believe it happened the way Ric had told it. He had heard things too much like it before and he figured Ric was exaggerating again. He would not be surprised, having watched the way Ric got down from the stool, if it had been Ric himself who got bounced down the stairs.

"What if?" Ric repeated.

"What if what?"

"All right. What if the Jew dies?"

Angie bolted away from him and outside. The Jew wasn't going to die, not because of Angie, but Ric had given him the shivers all the same.

Alice was waiting, the key in the lock. "Come on, Fat Boy. Time to go night-night." Angie wished she'd stop riding him.

Ric lumbered through the doorway. "Some Brother you

are," he said to Angie, and to the girl: "Thanks for the hospitality."

"Keep the change." She never let up.

Angie watched him go. He looked fatter than ever where his sweater bunched around his middle. He had his hands almost in his pockets, but they didn't fit all the way.

"The big slob," the girl said.

Angie said, "Thanks for standing up for me. I mean when I said about taking you home."

"Don't you want to?"

"I've never been in the Bronx."

"I don't live in the Bronx anymore. Come on." She hooked her arm in his. "I'll sew those cuffs up for you and iron them, and maybe tomorrow you'll change your mind and take me to Palisades Park. You really aren't going to California now, are you? The truth."

"I might."

"Do you actually have a plane ticket?"

"Uh-huh."

They walked in silence, crossing Houston Street with the traffic light. He didn't ask where she lived, he only tried to keep his step in time with hers. He was a little taller than her when you allowed for the way her hair was puffed up. It was the color of a half-ripe orange under the street lights. Every now and then she gave his arm a little squeeze. He responded by tightening his muscle.

"What made you say my name was Alice?"

"I don't know. Alice's Restaurant, I guess."

She squeezed his arm again. "I don't think I'd mind being an Alice. We'll look it up when we get home."

3 She lived on Sullivan Street in a basement apartment with bars on the small high windows and curtains of red, white, and blue polka dots. As soon as she yanked the curtains closed, she kicked off her shoes and started to take off her uniform. One look at Angie and she laughed, grabbed a garment from the beaverboard closet that separated the living room from the kitchen, and went into the bathroom in back. She called out to him to make himself at home.

Angie looked down at the shoes. They were swollen out of shape, like his mother's shoes, and he decided that Alice or whatever her name was must be a lot older than he had thought. One of the closet doors hung open the way she had left it. Angie picked up the shoes and took them to the closet where several other pairs in the same condition huddled on the floor. There was also a heap of soiled underwear, and, to Angie's shock, a man's suit. He took the shoes back and left them where he had found them.

He sat down on the daybed which rolled an inch or two from the wall. Then he got up and removed his coat. He folded it and left it on the bed and tried the chair underneath the lamp. A portable television set stared blankly at him, but he didn't think it would be polite to turn it on. There were books in the stand alongside the table. A dictionary and paperbacks with spooky titles and pictures of women lost in the woods. He had a feeling there wasn't an Italian name in any one of the books and began to search.

"Don't ask me how, but I just knew you were a bookworm,"

24

the girl said. She hung her uniform in the closet and closed the door. "Look up Alice in the back of the dictionary. I'll get us some wine. Do you like wine?"

"Sure."

In the dictionary he came first to the names of men. He knew what Angelo meant only too well. His second name was Carlo, Charles. It meant manly, strong.

Alice . . .

She came from the kitchen with a bottle and two glasses. She smelled of perfume. "So?"

"It means truth."

"Well now, isn't that interesting?"

"What?"

"That you should think I'm an Alice."

It wasn't that way at all, but he did not say so.

She put the glasses on the table and filled them with the dark wine. "*Skoal,*" she said, taking one glass and clicking it against the other.

"*Ciao,*" Angie said, and taking up the glass he sipped the wine. It was a surprise, sweeter than honey. "It's sweet."

"That's why I like it. It's kind of friendly when you get home at night. How old are you, Angie, if you don't mind me asking?"

"Nineteen." He wanted to say twenty-one but didn't have the nerve. "And you?"

She settled herself in the chair on the other side of the book stand, and tucked her feet under her. "It all depends," she said with a sigh. The robe came open when she leaned back and stretched. One of the big breasts came out. She covered it.

Angie shelved the dictionary, looking carefully to put it in the right place. He got a straight chair from across the room and straddled it, facing her, his arms on the chair back. "What's your real name?"

"Don't you like Alice?"

"Sure, but."

"Actually, I change it all the time," she said. "I don't think a person should keep anything they get tired of. And I don't think a person ought to do anything they don't want to. I'm a very independent person."

"Do you like working in a restaurant?"

"Sure I do. Except for my feet hurting sometimes. I get to meet all kinds of people."

"Men," Angie said.

"What's wrong with men? I don't *like* girls."

"I mean a certain kind of men." He was thinking of the truck driver sticking his tongue in his cheek to Angie.

"I like all kinds—except that Ric character. What makes you so scared of him?"

"I don't know." He couldn't explain what he felt about Ric, the inside fear: it wasn't so much of being hurt physically. It was something else, too. He stared at the wine where he had set it down on the table. "When we were little kids he used to get me down on the ground and he wouldn't let me up till I said I was his friend."

"Angie . . ." She waited for him to look at her. "Truth: you stole the coat, didn't you?"

"Yes."

"Do you think the person you stole it from will go to the police?"

"Maybe . . . I guess so." It seemed to have happened a long time before.

"Come on, tell Aunt Alice the whole story."

His eyes snapped and she laughed. She poured the wine he hadn't drunk into her glass. "I'm only teasing. You're so serious for an Italian."

"How did you know I was Italian?"

"I don't mind. I told you, I like all kinds of people unless they're mean. Was the fat boy with you when you stole the coat?"

"No. I got a place I go up on a roof and in the building across the street there's a girl . . ." He stopped. It was too hard to tell. "Let's forget about it, huh?"

"There's no harm in looking," Alice said, far ahead of him.

"If people leave their blinds up they got to expect it. It's a compliment in a way . . ."

So he managed to tell her what had happened from when the girl came to the window and pulled the shade down only to have it spring up to the top.

Alice thought about it and drank her wine. She licked in the purple traces around her mouth. "You'd been watching her before, right?"

"Sometimes."

"And him?"

"I never saw him before."

"So," she said. "Los Angeles. He's probably got a wife and kids at home."

"No!" It came out like a cry.

"Oh, boy," Alice said, "I sure get 'em with the hang-ups."

"To hell with you," Angie said, getting up. He pulled the chair from between his legs and set it down with a clatter. "No woman says that about a Sicilian."

"Mafia," she said, mocking him.

Angie charged across the room and grabbed up the coat. For a plumpish girl, Alice was very quick. She came up behind him, slipped her arms under his and around his middle. She locked him against her. He could feel the softness of her up and down him, the way her thighs fit under his buttocks, her belly in the small of his back, her breasts at his shoulderblades.

"Don't be mad at me, Angie," she said, and nipped his ear with her teeth. "I was only teasing. Would I 've asked you to come home with me if I didn't like you?" She wriggled her fingers through to where she could play with his nipples. Angie dropped the coat and grabbed her hands.

Alice laughed. "You do like me, don't you?"

"Sure."

"Don't you want to—you know?"

He said the word to himself. Aloud he murmured, "Sure."

She turned him around to her, letting the robe fall open and held him against her naked body. Angie tasted the wine in her

27

kiss, stronger than from the glass. She walked him slowly backwards until he collided with the daybed. He went down on his back, his legs sprawled and Alice on top of him, a delicious weight after the first stab of pain. She raised herself on knees and elbows and pushed the breasts up toward his face. He put his hand to one and the nipple hardened.

"Go on," she said. "That's what it's for."

He looked into her face; the wide eyes narrowed to shimmering slits, the sweat glistened on her upper lip. It was too much, a dream, and he thought of his mother and the fear of waking up to her accusation. Everything in him went limp. He turned his head aside. "I got to get up," he said.

He was ashamed to watch her move away, pulling the robe tight around her. The smell of her stayed with him, the wine, the perfume and the sweat, and he could hear her suck in her breath between her teeth.

"I'm sorry," he said. He swung his feet to the floor, and sitting, he put his face in his hands. He did not want to cry. Of all the things he didn't want to do at that moment, crying was foremost. From between his fingers he watched her pick up the sports jacket from the floor and hang it over a chair back. Don't let me cry, he prayed, then to himself he said, You goddamned wop, don't cry.

After a moment he heard voices. Alice had turned on the television. She wheeled it around and sat down beside him on the couch. She pulled one of his hands away from his face and held it in hers. "It's all right, baby," she said.

Baby.

"It's a good movie anyway," she said. "I've seen it a lot. *The Asphalt Jungle*."

Gradually, Angie became involved in the picture.

"I used to look like her," Alice said of the blond actress who didn't seem very bright to Angie.

"Who's she?"

"Marilyn Monroe."

"Is that Marilyn Monroe?"

"Yeah, that's her."

"You do look like her," Angie said, and squeezed her hand. There was not a strong resemblance.

After a while Alice put her arm around him and pulled his head down on her shoulder. He stayed that way even though it gave him a crick in the neck. His mind wandered from the picture to what had happened to him. It wasn't that he hadn't wanted to. He wondered if he should try to explain that to her. He wondered about the man's suit in the closet. Then he got caught up in the picture again. The burglars were moving into the jewelry shop. Doc ripped the sheet off a display case. Angie shivered. Alice gave his hair a tug. The shadows, the lookout, the footsteps, Doc lighting up a cigar—the sound of the electric drill as Louis revved the motor and put the drill to the safe lock. When the drill snapped, Alice laughed aloud.

On the screen Doc asked what happened. It broke, Louis said. He had another.

"Wow!" Alice said.

The sound of the drill again.

The scene changed to the Bellini kitchen. The wife and kid: Louis was Italian.

The scene changed to the crooked lawyer's wife: she was talking to herself about a pill.

Alice let go of Angie's head. "Stupid broad," she said, "and wait till you see the one coming up now."

Angie wasn't much interested in the lawyer's wife. He glanced at Alice: her robe was falling open again, little by little. He was fascinated to see if it would get stuck on the nipple—like it was a button.

To Doll, the girlfriend of one of the burglars, who was also talking to herself, Alice said, "Honey, what you don't know about men would fill a book. Tell him to go screw somewheres else!"

The action returned to the jewelry shop, the sound that of the drill. Louis stops at the sign from Doc. Everybody listens. Silence. Then the high, far-off whine of police sirens. Louis goes back to work. Doc smokes. Angie glanced again at Alice. The nipple was out. He felt her hand on his thigh, edging

29

higher and higher. The sirens drown out the sound of the drill. On screen, Doc says: How close are you now? Louis says, I'm packing it in.

Angie kept staring at the screen although he didn't really know what was going on there anymore—or anywhere else, exactly. Alice was on her knees on the floor in front of him, her face in the dark but her hair lighting up from the glare of the screen in the bright shots.

"Angie, you've never done it before, have you?"

He shook his head.

"Then just let yourself go, honey. Relax, and leave the driving to me."

"Angie? Are you asleep?"

He opened his eyes. The room was blue, a very dark blue, but outside it was daylight. "Sort of," he said. He wasn't. He was thinking of the Little Brothers, what had happened to him with Alice, and where it would fit in their code.

"Then wake up."

"I'm awake." There were patterns on the ceiling, white squares with circles that had curly shapes inside them. When he concentrated he could make faces out of them.

"I tell you what we'll do. Do you remember what time the plane's supposed to leave?"

"I don't think it says."

"What we'll do," Alice resumed, "at eight o'clock we'll take a taxi to the East Side terminal where all the airlines have ticket offices. I'll go up and say my brother got a ride back to California with somebody who was driving out there, and I'll ask them to refund the money."

Angie tried to picture this happening. "Who will they refund it to?"

"Me. Is there a name on the ticket?"

"Phillips."

"Then I'll say I'm Alice Phillips. Or I'll say Phillips was my maiden name in case they ask for identification. I'll say the trip is going to be much more educational for you . . . No. People do it all the time. I won't say anything, just that I want the money back. Was there anything else in the pockets?"

"No." Angie thought of the key, but didn't mention it. It might be to a locker in the terminal. He did not want to go any further than the plane ticket.

"I'll wear my gloves and my good purse. Wear something sensible, my mother always said. It'll be like looking for a job."

"What if he's already told the airline?" Angie asked.

"It's just tough luck, but that's why we're going right away, to be there first thing. I got a feeling he'll think it over for a while. I just hope it's a man that's working on the desk I have to go to."

Angie turned and looked down at her. Her side of the daybed was lower than his. "You sure do know a lot, Alice."

She pulled him down beside her, the frame of the bed a cold rod at his back. She locked her arms and legs around him. "Some day you're going to be a wonderful lover."

"Thanks," Angie said, not entirely happy.

"Look, honey, for the first time out . . ." She swung him off the bed onto the floor and got up, wrapping herself in the blanket. "We ought to get started. I'll make coffee as soon as I pee. Then you can have the bathroom."

Angie tried several expressions in the mirror over the sink while he washed. His eyes were bloodshot, but that didn't make him look older. Only sick. He saw Alice's razor on the shelf and felt his chin. As smooth as his behind. It was only the sports coat that made him look older. He went to the door. "Alice, what if he did go to the police? Wouldn't they check the airline? I wouldn't want you getting into trouble." He smelled the wool where she was pressing the sleeves of the jacket.

"I got it all figured out. That's why *I'm* taking back the ticket, not you. You don't even know me when we get there. Then, if anything goes wrong, I'll turn around and say I found the ticket on the restaurant floor when I was closing up last night. They can't blame a girl for trying to pick up a few bucks. It's free enterprise if you look at it that way."

4 In the terminal lobby they agreed to meet at the top of the escalator and then went off in opposite directions. As soon as Alice was out of sight, Angie looked for the public lockers. The key in his pocket bore the numeral 39, but it could be to a locker almost anywhere: so he warned himself unnecessarily. The locker sprang open before Angie had really made up his mind to turn the key. Inside was a black leather suitcase. Angie closed the door at once and put fifty cents in the slot. He got away from there as quickly as he could. He did not want Alice to think he was holding out on her, but he did not want to get in any deeper either.

He was waiting at the escalator when she came gliding up, all smiles. As soon as she landed she removed the big floppy hat she'd decided to wear and pushed her hair up as high as it would go.

"Perfectly simple," she said as they left the building. "They wanted to send us a check, but I said the cash was important because you wanted to pay your share of the gasoline."

"I would," Angie said.

She looked at him as though he wasn't all there. She moved into stride. "Now we'll find a nice restaurant and have breakfast. I want to leave the waitress a big tip." She hooked her arm through his. "We're going to have a lovely time."

He tried to stay in step with her. "Alice, whose suit is it, the one hanging in your closet?"

"Oh, just a friend's. He's in the army now, in Japan or some place."

"Wouldn't he mind—you and me, I mean?"

She laughed. "Honey, you got to realize, I'm not exclusive. What I mean is, maybe he'll get killed over there, and I wouldn't want *him* waiting to come home. Like waiting for me exclusively. Besides, I know he wouldn't, and if he finds some nice geisha girl, that's fine with me. Then when he comes back, we'll see. It's no big deal to take a suit of clothes out of a closet."

Angie thought about it, and he thought again of the girl on Mulberry Street and the man whose coat he was wearing. "How much money did you get, Alice?"

"I was waiting for you to ask. A hundred and forty-nine dollars."

Angie's first thought was what if he ever had to pay it back? but all he said was "Wow."

They walked to Fifth Avenue which was her favorite street and then crossed and recrossed it so that she could look in the windows of Altman's, Lord and Taylor, Arnold Constable. Angie kept seeing his own reflection, the smooth sports jacket and the bluejeans. At least she'd fixed the cuffs so that he didn't look like a circus clown. Across from the Public Library, Angie said, "I've been in there."

"You got a real thing on books, don't you?"

"Books and movies. Would you like to go to a movie? You could maybe say you're sick and take the night off . . ."

She giggled. "We got television at home. Remember?"

He didn't think he would ever forget it, but he didn't say anything.

"You're so funny," she said. "I didn't think there was anybody as bashful as you anymore."

"Maybe there isn't. I mean I'm different."

"That's what I mean."

She chose Stouffer's Restaurant and asked for a table by the window. Angie felt more at ease when he was seated opposite her, his sneakers and jeans concealed beneath the table. Alice groped for his knee and gave it a squeeze that made him jump.

"Silly, take it," she said.

33

Angie put his hand to hers and discovered that she was trying to give him a wad of money. He took it and, without looking, stuffed it in his pocket.

"Now, how do you feel?"

"Better," Angie said.

A dream inside a dream inside a dream: how far down the tunnel could you go without coming out in your own room? But if he had been dreaming, he couldn't see how a girl like Alice would show up there. He'd never known anyone like her. The tunnel idea came from the fact that they were walking through the long passageway in the Port Authority Bus Terminal, past news stands, donut shops, hamburger stands, gift shops, trying to get to where they could buy a ticket for a bus that would take them to the Palisades Park. Angie would still have preferred Coney Island no matter what the class of people. He had only been across the Hudson River once in his life, to visit his Uncle Dom's chicken farm. He couldn't remember much about it except the smell.

He kept wishing his mother would wake him up. Only she wasn't going to: he knew that. What he ought to do was telephone her at the bakery: he would say he stayed the night with a friend. She'd want to ask him questions, but not on the phone. Her boss would be listening.

As they were passing a Ladies Room Alice said, "I'd better pop in here for a minute. They don't have johns on buses."

The idea of a long bus trip and then her suddenly leaving him alone in a place he had never been before made Angie want to cut out and run, to lose Alice from his life forever. But he had in his hand the shopping bag they had bought to carry her hat in and for all the prizes she expected to win that afternoon. Not very far away was a row of phones. He decided to call the bakery, and so that Alice would spot him when she came out, he left the shopping bag at his feet, facing the Ladies Room. You couldn't very well miss it, red, white, and blue stars with the face of a movie personality in every star.

The phones weren't very private, with only glass partitions

in between, but other people did not seem to mind. Angie dialed and waited. The phone was ringing but the shop was busy at this time of day. In the next stall, the man was reading a newspaper while he listened to whoever was on the other end of the phone; Angie could hear him say "Yeah" every once in a while. It was on the page facing Angie that the boy noticed the heading: "Shopkeeper Knifed To Death in Lower East Side Hallway."

The whole building seemed to tip, Angie going over with it. He could hear his mother shouting "Hello" into the phone. That voice steadied him. When she hung up, he hung up too. He leaned closer to the partition and read a few words before his eyes went bleary: "Benjamin Grossman, a man considered . . ."

5 The ranking detective on the scene, Lieutenant David Marks of Homicide and the precinct man, Sergeant Gerald Regan, stopped talking when they saw the blond girl approach the police barricade. She shaded her eyes to better see what was going on inside. Marks glanced at Regan who had just got through saying he knew the neighborhood like the back of his hand: he'd ought to, having spent most of his twenty years on the force there. Regan's face registered a sour approval of what he saw. In a kind of chain reaction, the men working within the shop stopped, one by one, to have a look. Wally Herring, a black detective who, with a narcotics man, had been smashing the statuettes, ran his tongue over his lips and had, then, to spit. He was in white face from the dust.

"Local product?" Marks asked, indicating the girl.

"I've seen her around," Regan said, not committing himself.

The patrolman on duty outside went up to her, touched his cap, and asked her to move on.

"Damn fool rookie," Regan said of his own man.

The young woman walked away with an exquisite erectness which her shaggy shorts and tailored blouse only emphasized. It was the kind of angular beauty that got to Marks.

"That's a chick with too much gristle for me," Herring said. Most of the men agreed.

Marks stepped outdoors in time to see her go into the delicatessen. Detective Tomasino was in there so Marks turned his attention once more to the clean square in the plate glass window. He kept trying to figure out what it meant. For all the technical attention already paid it, the measurements of angles of vision, photography of and through the glass, Marks went back to his own calculations. If the square had been made in order that someone could better see inside the store, that someone was not much over five feet tall. If it was made to erase an obscenity—he was thinking of the swastikas newly scrawled on the hallway walls—traces of the marker ought to have shown under power photography. The natural way to go about cleaning a spot in a dirty window, or to rub something out, would be to use a roughly circular motion. To Marks this was a window within a window, but what did it mean?

So far there were no witnesses. Nobody wanted to talk about Grossman, not even those who liked to talk and presumably trusted the precinct men who went round with the detectives for good will. Perhaps that was the trouble: too much good will. Marks had felt from the moment he arrived that the shop was a cover and the discovery on the premises of a good deal of money reinforced that belief. If it were so, the precinct men ought to have known it. Regan said that himself, but what Marks had to bear in mind about Regan was that he was a precinct man. When the Commissioner of Police had abolished the precinct detectives in favor of district squads of specialists, Regan, a former detective first grade, chose to go back into uniform and settle for his sergeant's stripes and a locker in the old stationhouse.

Marks hunched his six feet down to five and studied what came within his line of vision. The display counter; there was not even a cash register, only a tin box on the back shelf with its few dollars in change untouched. He could plainly see the wall safe, now open, but which, on the arrival of the police, had been closed and concealed behind a rolltop desk. A watcher would have seen only the desk. A back panel to the desk was removable. The safe had contained over eighty thousand dollars in small bills which Marks doubted would yield any useful information to the Treasury Department tracers.

The question raised by the large amount of money, so far as

Homicide was concerned, went to whether or not it was left intentionally. If it was, a practice common to the Mafia, it suggested "family" involvement. If it remained in the safe because the assailant did not know it was there, what was the motive? Nor was Grossman attacked in the shop: it appeared that his assailant had waited for him to close the shop. The attack had occurred outside the door to his second-floor apartment.

Marks went indoors again. Regan muttered something about having to get back to the stationhouse and yet he could not bring himself to leave. The word cooperation had been flung about all morning like confetti at a wedding: in former days Regan would have been in charge. Marks had asked him, as soon as they sprung the safe combination and counted the money, where he would start. Loan sharking. Which was why, when he had to speak to the reporters on hand, Marks had suggested that Grossman might have died a rich man: he hoped that money might smoke out witnesses. He had little faith himself in Regan's theory. There was neither ledger nor pledges among Grossman's meager effects.

Regan picked up the *Post* which a technician had brought in with him. "It says here he was a violinist. Where the hell did they get that information?"

"Not from me," Marks said.

"The rest is gobbledygook." It was a word Marks had not heard since his youth. Regan turned to the sports page. Marks wished he would go. No. What he actually wished was that he had not come himself. It was Tomasino, a very competent young detective, who had answered the complaint. The case should have rightly remained his, but the combination of swastikas in the hallway and the tattooed numerals of the Nazi concentration camp on the victim's wrist had prompted Tomasino to call in his superior. Which irritated Marks, an irrational response; by the same token, Tomasino could ask why *he* had been dispatched to Little Italy.

Marks was irritated with himself, that was the trouble. He had fallen into a lugubrious exchange with Regan in which he wound up saying that some of the greatest bastards he knew came out of the concentration camps, that it went with survival; but what it sounded like was his saying that any Jew with a number on his arm was probably a bastard. Grossman had been the only Jewish merchant on the block, and the fact that his ostensible wares were religious articles, Roman and Orthodox Catholic, only made things stickier.

Regan was finally half-way out the door when Tomasino appeared with the blond girl in tow. He made way for them to enter by stepping back into the shop himself, and of course he stayed.

"This is Miss Julie Borghese," Tomasino said. "She saw Grossman at eleven-thirty last night, alive and kicking his cat." He introduced Marks and Regan.

In view of the fact that the cat had been killed along with its master, Marks said, "Actually kicking it?"

"Oh, yes. He frequently kicked it. I threatened him once with calling the ASPCA." Her speech placed her origins far from the Lower East Side. "He said it was none of my business. Did I butt into every family quarrel in the neighborhood? Maybe it was a family affair. No matter what he did to it, the cat always came back for more."

The Stranger," Marks said, thinking of the dog-master relationship in a favorite novel of his own youth. He would not have readily admitted that he said it to impress the girl. Tomasino, who had his notebook out, omitted this exchange.

"Possibly," she said.

"Possibly what?" Regan said.

"A love-hate relationship," the girl said.

Regan puffed out his cheeks in a way that effectively conveyed what he thought of love-hate relationships.

Tomasino took down the correct spelling of her name and her address.

"Do you live alone, Miss Borghese?" Marks asked.

"Sometimes."

Detective Herring had dusted an appropriately sized space in the window dais.

"Sit down, if you like," Marks said, offering the clean spot. "Are you Italian?" He asked it lightly, knowing it to be none of his business. He did not want to come right out and say she didn't go with her Mulberry Street address.

"My father is of Italian extraction."

"His address?"

"I am twenty-one years old," she said, and sat down with confident ease.

"Occupation?"

"Mine or my father's?"

"Which do you live on?" Marks said.

"I am an actress."

"Will you tell us in your own words how you happened to be here at eleven-thirty last night, and what it was you saw?"

First she amended: "I'm not the greatest actress. I study acting. Sometimes I get a day's work or so. Yesterday and last night I worked on the picture *Grand Street*, which they're shooting on location. At eleven o'clock we broke. I had to get out of costume. I wore a wig, you see, because everybody knows there are no blond Italians . . ."

Tomasino wrote it down, grinning.

"On my way home I stopped at the deli which I almost always do," she went on, "and then I looked in on Mr. Grossman which I sometimes do—did."

"What do you mean by 'looked in' "?

"I opened the door and said 'Hi.' He turned around and the cat was in his way. He kicked it aside. I said to him, 'You're a mean bastard and they'll get back at you,' meaning the cats. I have a very strong feeling about cats. They're the next civilization. Something got mixed up in evolution so that we came before they were ready. Think about the sphinxes."

Tomasino frowned and scratched out the last few sentences.

Marks said, "Miss Borghese, have you looked in the shop from outside the window itself lately?"

She knew what he was getting at. "Yes. I looked in through that patch of daylight the other day." She glanced over her shoulder at the clean place. "It caught my attention and I looked in. That's all."

That, Marks thought, was normal procedure, even as people look in on excavations where provision has been made for the curious. He questioned her on the date. Then, "How did he respond to your calling him a bastard?"

"He said, 'You wouldn't believe how many people agree with you.' "

"Do you remember the first time you came into the shop?"

"Yes. It's almost a year ago. I was furnishing my apartment and I came in to buy a picture."

"A religious picture?"

"Yes, lieutenant, a religious picture."

Marks knew the silent Regan was pleased. Until now Julie would not have entirely satisfied his notion of a nice girl. Her defense of something sacred gave her a whole new dimension.

Then Julie opened up. "Look, officers, we sometimes talked. Once he told me about the Yiddish Theatre in Berlin before Hitler. Another time—he admired discipline, and we got into a crazy hassle about it. To me it's crap, you know? I leaned over and touched the tattoo mark on his arm. 'That's discipline,' I said. 'I am here today. That, too, is discipline,' he said. So what? Do two disciplines make one freedom? Do two deaths make one life, you know?"

Marks smiled. He wasn't sure whether she was making him feel older or younger than he was. "Why was Grossman here, in this particular shop, in this location, do you know?"

She shook her head. "I don't think he was here because he wanted to be . . . I shouldn't say that because I just don't know. It's a feeling. He didn't like it here much, but I don't know where he would have liked. Maybe Berlin in 1929. He especially did not like the teen-aged boys. He called them baby fascists."

"Did he say why he didn't like them?"

"They tormented him. They tried to extort money from him."

41

"That's a pretty big word, miss," Regan said.

"Did you like Grossman?" Marks asked.

"Except for the way he treated the cat, I kind of dug him. But *like?* That's a pretty big word, lieutenant." She mimicked Regan's tone.

"Did he ever speak about music?"

Julie shook her head. "But then I'm not very musical."

"I wonder how the newspapers get information we can't get," Marks said to no one in particular.

"Because the people trust them," Julie said sweetly.

Regan had had enough. He offered Marks his hand. "We'll have room for you over there if you need it, lieutenant. It's an old-fashioned station, strong on history, weak in plumbing. The taxpayers are a sentimental lot."

He saluted Julie and left.

In the few seconds of silence that fell throughout the shop with his departure, Marks could hear the creak of the floorboards overhead where the search of Grossman's apartment continued. He heard also a sound like the gnawing of rats.

"What's that?" the girl asked, hearing it too.

"It's our lab people," Tomasino said. "They're scraping the floorboards for specimens."

"It takes a long time to find out something that way, doesn't it?"

"Yes, but it's information you can rely on."

He watched Tomasino walk her back to the delicatessen. They both looked so young. Tomasino was engaged to be married. Marks was himself a bachelor of long standing.

He went outdoors and around to the hallway. While he observed the delicate process of lifting a square of ancient wallpaper, he thought about the Alberto Ruggio family who lived on the third floor, father, mother, and infant child. Could they find no better housing than this? Marks had not been present at the questioning of Ruggio, who had discovered the body when he was leaving for work at seven-thirty that morning. Not that his presence would have greatly improved the quality of the interrogation, especially in this instance, where the statement had been translated from Italian. He simply felt that something was missing from his personal docket that loosened his grasp of the case. He wanted a face-to-face meeting with Ruggio soon.

An Italian immigrant of just under a year's residence in the United States, Ruggio worked as a truck loader for the Ambrose Corporation, an importer of Italian foods. He had learned of the Grossman apartment from a mechanic where he worked. Grossman, according to the statement, had not wanted to rent to him because of the infant. Marks wondered how he had been persuaded: it was not in the testimony. Grossman frequently complained of the child's crying.

The only toilet in the building was on the second floor, the only light on that floor came from there. A gas jet in the hall had never been replaced. Presumably with the commode door closed, the floor was in darkness. The window had been boarded up.

The man had stumbled over the body that morning, panicked, started to run downstairs, then, remembering that they had had a phone installed only that week, he had reversed himself and gone back upstairs. It was then that he saw the cat, stiffer by far than the human victim.

The immigrant's shoes had been sent to the laboratory. It was a question of whether a discrepancy might show up in his story, that he might have been on the death site at different hours, this to be possibly determined by a variance in the coagulation of the blood stains on his shoes. Marks could plainly hear the baby crying, one flight up. Did Grossman make no sound when attacked? Nor the cat, that the family should sleep through such violence? He sidled by the technicians and went up to try his luck with Mrs. Ruggio despite the inadequacy of his Italian.

A sturdy girl finally opened the door to him. The baby lay squalling on the couch where she had put it down, needing both hands to manage the door. There was fear in her eyes and the wariness of body had suggested a readiness to put herself between him and the child, and yet she did not pick it up. Her hand fumbled at the top buttons of her blouse which was open. He felt something go out of his mind as the child's crying persisted and the woman did nothing about it.

"Take him up!" Marks said, making the gesture to reinforce the words. The infant wore only diapers.

"Police?" the woman asked, still rooted.

"Yes! Si!" He pulled out his identification and showed her the photograph.

She looked at it and made sure. Then she picked the child up who immediately groped, hand and mouth, for a breast. She went to a table where a fresh supply of diapers was laid out, and arranged one to conceal the breast and much of the baby's head.

What interested Marks the most was that while she was afraid, it apparently was not of the police.

Marks said "Please" when she returned, and motioned toward the rocker near the window. He stood by the window himself and looked out most of the time. The baby made more noise sucking than Marks would have thought possible. Inadvertently he glanced toward the mother.

"Pig," she said. Then hastily: "Him, him. Not you."

That much of the modern American idiom she had picked up. "Him *and* me," Marks said, with a sigh. Across the way was a leathergoods factory, but there was no one at the benches. He recalled that it was closed for vacation. He turned back to the room. It was bare and clean. Shallow roots. And no wonder, if this was the best America had to offer. He could see through to the kitchen and the old-fashioned tub. On the living room table was one of Grossman's statuettes—of a sorrowing male saint. All Grossman's statues and icons were made in Italy. There was a candle burning before this one, the wax scented. The sweet smell was pervasive.

"How long are you in America?"

"One year."

"In this apartment?"

"Nice," she said, so that he let it go without knowing whether or not she had understood him. There was a pillow at his feet. Like most of the ghetto women, she was a street watcher. He leaned out the window: much of the street was obscured from that vantage by the green, white, and red streamers. Beneath him he saw the laboratory truck pull away. A block away was the Bowery, and on the other side, what most people had in mind when they spoke of the Lower East Side, one of the most famous Jewish ghettos in the world. Why did Grossman settle on Hester Street, west of the Bowery?

Mrs. Ruggio was buttoning her blouse when Marks pulled back into the room. The child was finishing off on his own thumb.

"What's his name?"

"Francesco." She turned and pointed to the statue.

"St. Francis?"

"Si." She smiled.

Marks strode across the room, picked up the statuette—not roughly, but there was no gentle way to make this move—tumbled it back and forth, and sounded it with a tap of his fingernail. His main purpose was to get a reaction out of the woman, to perhaps touch that nerve end of fear again. She watched him without a change in expression: not surprise, not anger, not fear. Which was in itself unnatural. He put the saint back in his place and returned to her side. He harkened back to her original response on seeing him in the doorway. "What are you afraid of, Mrs. Ruggio?"

"Afraid?" she repeated.

She knew damn well what he meant. Marks drew his hand back as though he were going to strike her. She pulled away, turning her face from him. He waited. When she looked at him again, he said. "That's afraid," he said and pointed to her. He repeated his question, with one alteration: "*Who* are you afraid of?"

"America," she said, and looked him in the eye.

He had no choice but to take it for an answer.

On his way downstairs he stopped in on the team working

over Grossman's apartment. Nothing in the way of personal papers had shown up on the premises, not a bankbook, lease or mortgage to the building, no lading bills on the merchandise, nothing. "There's got to be a bank deposit box somewhere, boss," one of the men said.

"Find it and get us a court order," Marks said.

Tomasino was waiting for him at the bottom of the stairs. "Dave, here's something interesting: Allioto, the delicatessen owner? He says that when Miss Borghese came in there last night she had a man with her. Now why wouldn't she 've mentioned him to us?"

"Let's find out. What else have we got to do?"

Tomasino understood the shortness, the impatience of Marks, of indeed any officer in charge of a homicide investigation that seemed likely to depend more on technical than human evidence, and most cases did.

"I thought it might be you," Julie said through an inch or so of doorway. She removed the latch chain and allowed the two detectives to enter.

A man stood at the window, his back to them. Marks was aware of him, but the first thing he actually saw on entering the room—his eyes could not escape it—was the religious picture. It hung on the wall directly opposite the door. Marks wished Regan was with them. A blue-robed madonna was pictured floating, he presumed heavenwards, on a cushion of cloud. The print had been mounted on cardboard, with the words WOMEN'S LIB lettered in red underneath.

Julie called out quite unnecessarily, "Sorry, Mike, but they're here in person."

The man remained at the window.

Marks said, "Any particular reason you didn't mention your companion to us, Miss Borghese?"

"He did not go into Mr. Grossman's with me."

The man joined them in his own good time. Julie introduced him. "This is Michael Phillips, Lieutenant Marks, and—I'm sorry, I don't remember . . ."

"Pasquale Tomasino, Detective First Grade," Tomasino clipped the words.

Phillips did not offer to shake hands, nor did the detectives. He was good-looking in a weak sort of way; a beardless face with very smooth skin made it hard to guess his age. There was something . . . off about him, Marks felt; something institutional; the idea of prison went through his mind. Phillips gave Julie's address as his also, and added: "Temporarily."

"Do you have a permanent address, Mr. Phillips?"

"3897 Granada Vista, Los Angeles."

"Occupation?"

"Sometimes I edit film."

"And other times you don't," Marks said.

"You're right, lieutenant." There was a suggestion of martyrdom in the quiet way he said it, something that made Marks feel like a bully. He turned the questioning over to Tomasino who had his notebook in hand.

While he listened, Marks appraised Julie by the house she kept. It was very neat, which was fortunate, considering the number of objects in the one room and kitchen apartment. It confirmed the background he had suspected: a loom stood in the corner like an attic ghost. Alongside it, a cased guitar; there was a microscope in a plastic hood on top of the bookcase, and the bookcase itself was stacked with expensive art and film books too large to shelve upright. The paperbacks included Paul Goodman, Jerry Rubin, Eldridge Cleaver, and on the end, where he glowered from the jacket like a child determined not to grow up, Norman Mailer. On the table were several public library books—politics of the left, women's rights, Che Guevera . . . Julie would have parents of means who had indulged her shifting interests—up to the point of political activism. The detective wondered if Phillips belonged in that set-up, if possibly he was on the run.

Phillips himself responded carefully to Tomasino's question as to whether he would recognize any of the four or five people who passed while he waited outside Grossman's for Julie. "I might, but I don't think it would be useful."

"Why not?"

"A good lawyer could take apart such identification. The street isn't well lighted."

"You're jumping the gun on us, Mr. Phillips," Marks said over his shoulder. "Before we can go to trial we need a charge, and before we can make a charge we need a suspect. It might be one of those people."

"It is possible I could make tentative identification of one or two persons."

Marks kept wandering around the room: he saw no evidence of this man's residence with Julie. He had no warrant to search, and no reason in terms of the homicide. Yet he was curious. Why, if Phillips had any possible reason for avoiding the authorities, did he admit to seeing anyone outside the shop at all?

Tomasino asked for descriptions.

"One was a rather plump young man—I think he was young. In any case, he walked with a rolling gait like a sailor's."

"What do you see, lieutenant?" Julie asked. She had been watching Marks with a look of amused detachment.

"Not much I didn't expect to see, except for one thing, Miss."

"Yes?"

"Your partner's gear." He nodded toward Phillips.

"Have you really looked?" she said, meeting his eyes dead on.

Marks spun around on his heel. "As soon as you're ready, Tommy."

6 Angie prayed that Alice would not come out until he could get away. He stripped two of the bills from the money folded in his pocket and stuffed them into the bottom of the shopping bag. Then he opened the door to the Ladies Room without looking inside and threw the bag through the doorway. Somebody screamed, but Angie bolted from the waiting room into the concourse and pushed into a stream of people. He let it carry him toward the street. His body oozed a cold sweat and he could smell its taint of sickness.

"Angeeeee!" Alice's voice filled the concourse. He did not look back. He kept his head down and stayed to the middle of the crowd. He didn't know when Alice stopped screaming his name; the noise in his own head throbbed louder. He tried not to push and he did not look around. He hoped she would look in the bag soon. He didn't even know why he had run away from her, except that alone, he could run faster. But what he needed was someone to tell, someone to help him figure out . . . What he needed was to get rid of the coat which was making him sweat so much. What he needed was to wake up and find out it was all a nightmare.

The crowd carried him out with them onto Eighth Avenue where he could not get his sense of direction, first going downtown when he thought he was going uptown; changing his mind, he kept bumping into people. He tripped over a leash between a man and his dog and both of them snapped at him. I didn't, I didn't, he kept saying to himself. But then, why did it happen? It had to have something to do with Ric, the way he showed up at the restaurant and how he looked. It was Ric Angie wanted dead, not Mr. Grossman, really.

At the corner of Forty-second Street he bought a paper. He'd never bought one before and the man had to tell him how much it cost. Angie went a few storefronts along and then tried to find the story. His hands shook so much he could hardly turn the pages. A guy with a scraggle of beard was watching him in the store window. Their eyes met. Angie closed the paper and fled. The street was wild, even at noon. Kids roamed in gangs, high on drugs or something. Then there were men lolling in doorways, making dirty remarks, and women talking to themselves. Boys minced in high-heeled boots, some wore earrings, some even make-up like girls, and all of them kept looking after him and whistling. The cops walked in pairs, their radios crackling. On half the movie marquees the word Naked was in the title. Angie chose one where the lobby lights were the brightest. He could read the paper after he calmed down, then in the darkened theater he could close his eyes and think what he ought to do.

He pushed two dollars through the slot to the cashier. She was about to take the money when she changed her mind and shook her head. Behind Angie, a cop had come up from nowhere. Angie's tongue felt like a ball of wool.

"How old are you, son?"

"Sixteen," he managed.

"Got anything on you to prove it?"

He shook his head.

"Does your mother know where you are?"

Again he shook his head.

"Then get the hell home out of here. This is no place for a kid like you."

Angie started away.

"Hey!"

He froze.

"Don't let me catch you sneaking into some other dive."

Angie bobbed his head that he understood and went on. God, God, God. What made him look so different today that a

50

cop could pick him out. The coat? And he'd thought all the time it made him look older. Or did he look guilty, scared? He'd been on Forty-second Street lots of times before and nobody'd paid any attention to him.

He trudged on, the midday sun on his head and his back and more heat coming up at him from the pavement. In a sporting goods shop he caught sight of a knife just like his. He hadn't looked for it, it was like it was there waiting for him to pass. He had to find a place where he could read the paper.

He came then to Bryant Park in back of the Public Library. People were eating their lunches, pigeons swarming around them. Fat old ladies seemed to spread themselves out to keep other people from sitting on the benches. Angie found himself a place in the shade on the steps. He opened the paper. The birds waddled up. "Please, go away," he said. At last he found the story. He read:

> Benjamin Grossman, a man considered mysterious and hostile by his neighbors, was found stabbed to death this morning in the hallway of the building where he owned a religious articles shop at 1144 Hester Street. The body was discovered by Alberto Ruggio, the third-floor tenant, as he was leaving for work. Grossman lived alone, except for his cat, on the second floor of the building. A macabre aspect to the case is that the cat also had been knifed to death. Lieutenant David Marks of the Homicide Division speculated that Grossman's assailant might have waited on the second floor until the shopkeeper closed around midnight, and then surprised him at the top of the stairs.
>
> Grossman, who bore the numerals of the Nazi concentration camp on his arm, was a familiar if solitary figure in the neighborhood. Some of the older residents remember him working as a custodian and watchman in the warehouses that scatter the district. In the early 1960's he opened the shop which deals in religious articles. He is supposed at one time, to have been a violinist. It is also rumored that he died a rich man. However, robbery does not seem to have been the motive for the crime.

Angie read the article twice, losing track both times after the sentence about the cat.

The pigeons would not let him alone, stalking back and forth in front of him. One pecked at his sneaker. He kicked out at it. It skittered away and then waddled back. He folded the paper open to the story and set it on the steps while he took off the jacket. The air on his sweat-soaked shirt set him to shivering again.

"You shouldn't kick any living thing," a woman's voice said.

He looked around and saw first her shoes, sneakers in worse condition than his own, and wrinkled stockings twisted into garters at her knees. She came down slowly, putting both feet on one step before taking the next. Her dress was a pattern of faded butterflies, and she carried a dirty shopping bag which she set down next to Angie before she settled herself on the newspaper.

"You shouldn't," she repeated.

"I know."

The birds now came in swarms, sparrows and starlings as well as the pigeons. She was old and her skin was shriveled and rough with two high spots of rouge on her cheeks. Her eyes were pale blue and red-rimmed from tearing. She imitated the bird sounds, and reached into the bag from which she took a handful of seeds. Instead of scattering them, she held her hand out to Angie.

"You feed them."

Angie cupped his hands and tried to hold them steady. The seeds trickled into them. She made him wait for another of her handsful. He tossed the seeds out as he might a basketball, in one motion. The birds flew off in all directions.

"Not that way!" the old woman said, and with a flick of her wrist each time, she demonstrated with empty fingers a gentler motion which somehow suggested that the birds would share and share alike. "They'll come back." She folded her hands and waited, glancing at Angie sideways.

"Are you Jewish?"

"Italian."

"Mmmmmmm," she said without enthusiasm. Then with sudden brightness: "Do you sing?"

"No, ma'am."

"What do you do?"

"I dance," Angie said. It was all so crazy.

"I used to dance." She braced herself on her elbows, leaning on the step behind her and stuck her feet out straight and off the ground. "You wouldn't believe it, but inside those somewhat disreputable shoes is a pair of exquisite feet."

"I believe it," Angie said. He was afraid she would take off her shoes to show him. People were looking at them.

"The *entrechat* six: do you know what that is?"

"Sort of."

"Sort of. What kind of an answer is that?" She crossed her ankles and let her feet rest in front of her. She looked at him sharply. "Are you ill?"

"To tell you the truth, I don't feel very good," he said. His teeth were beginning to chatter. He ground them together.

"You look consumptive. Are you poor?"

"Sort of," he said again.

"You are either poor or you're not poor. I am rich but unconventional. I live in a mansion on Tenth Avenue and Twenty-first Street. Remember that if ever you are destitute. It is not a fit condition for any living thing."

Angie put on the coat again. He thought of trying to run, but that would look funny. Besides, he wanted the newspaper and she was sitting on it.

"What lovely material," she said, and put out her scruffy hand to stroke the sleeve. It reminded him of Ric in Alice's restaurant.

Angie groaned and then without warning that it was going to happen, he found himself sobbing. He buried his face in his hands and wept, unable to control himself.

"Dear, dear, dear . . ." The woman patted at him. Then she pulled at his shoulder. She pushed the bag from between them and sidled along the step. "There, there, young man. Look at the birds! Greedy things."

53

The bag had spilled and the birds came swarming.

"Please, please go away and leave me," Angie pleaded. He could not stop crying.

"In a state like this? I certainly will not. Listen to me. Do you hear?"

He nodded without raising his head.

"Do you have any money?"

He patted his pocket where the money was.

"Then you can take me to lunch and we'll get you some nice hot soup. There's a Chockful o' Nuts across the street. They're very rude to me, but they won't be when I'm with you. I'm very hungry, but I spent all the money I had with me for the children. And you kicked one of them."

"I didn't mean to," Angie said. He wiped his eyes on his sleeve and squeezed them tight to keep the tears from starting again.

"We never mean to, but we always do," she said severely.

"Just shut up a minute," he said. "Excuse me. I didn't mean to say that, only . . ." He let the words go and worked a bill from among the others in his pocket. Without looking, even as happened with Alice, he gave the woman the money.

Her hand gobbled it faster than the birds the seed and in the one motion vanished it in her bosom. "Do come and see me," she said. She got to her feet a lot faster than she'd been able to sit down. Angie just closed his eyes. He did not want to see her anymore.

"Mag . . ." The warning male voice of authority told Angie it was a policeman. He opened his eyes and saw the black officer, his night stick dangling from his hand. "I promised you a summons for feeding the pigeons, Mag."

"But I didn't, officer. The young man fed them, but he didn't know . . ."

"Take off, Mag, before I open my book."

The cop turned his attention to Angie. "On your feet, kid. Put your hands at the back of your head."

Angie obeyed him. He was cured of his tears. The old

woman scuttled away. But people were moving in on all sides around him and the cop.

"How much did you give her?"

He did not know. He said, "A dollar."

"What's the matter with you? What's giving you the shakes?" The cop turned him around gingerly and ran his hand over him for weapons.

"I got a chill, that's all," Angie said. "I'm just getting over the flu."

"Is that a fact? Turn out your pockets."

A white cop came toward them, pushing through the people.

Angie turned out the coat pockets. There was only the key. It did not fall out, but he was afraid the cop might find it anyway so he fished it out himself. "My locker key."

"The pants pockets," the black cop ordered.

Angie tried to put the money in his coat pocket when he took it out. The cop stayed his arm with the stick. "How much?"

"What did I do? I just gave the old beggar a dollar." It was his first feeble attempt at self-defense.

"How much?" the cop repeated.

"I don't know."

"You don't know?"

"I haven't counted it lately. That's all."

"Count it."

Angie's fingers trembled so much the bills slipped back on one another. He got to thirty and had to start over.

"Where'd it come from?"

"Forty-two dollars . . . It's my graduation money." Graduation in August.

"Say 'sir' to me," the cop said.

The white cop stood by, his legs apart, his arms folded.

The black cop examined Angie's arms up to the shoulders. Then Angie knew what it was all about. Drugs. The cop was examining him for needle scars. Who wouldn't think it, the money, the shakes? Except if he needed a fix, would he be giving away the money to the old woman?

The policeman lectured him about taking care of himself and not showing off his money. Then they let him go. They scattered the people the way the people scattered the birds. Angie made his way around the library to Fifth Avenue. What he didn't know about uptown was more than he did know about downtown. A longing to go home came over him, then another wave of fear. And he had lost the newspaper. A violinist. Mr. Grossman? That was harder to believe than anything. Maybe it was another Grossman . . . That fantasy fell apart before he could add a thing to it: Hester Street, the cat, religious articles. What did the Little Brothers think when they heard? Or did they already know?

Hail Mary, full of grace . . . Angie found himself going back the way he and Alice had come that morning: he felt it was a good sign, somebody giving directions. He wasn't just wandering anymore. The first thing he ought to do, in case he decided to go home later, was get rid of the coat. He could put it in the locker with the suitcase and then get the locker key to the man. He would figure out how later.

When he reached the bus terminal and heard the departures announced—one bus was connecting with two different flights to Los Angeles—he wished again that he had the plane ticket. He wished his brother, Pietro, who was in the marines, was still at San Diego. He had written Angie from there. He had seen their father who told him he could come and work in the orange groves after he got out of service. Angie could work in the orange groves if Pietro could. But first he had to get there.

He wished the suitcase was full of money, that it belonged to a bank robber. Then he thought of the girl and took the wish back. He opened the locker and pulled the suitcase out. It was so light the coat would fit inside. He tried the clasp and it sprang open. He took out the suitcase and set it on the floor while he took off the coat and folded it. Then he opened the suitcase. A couple of changes of underwear and white shirts . . . without collars, then tucked in at the side, two stiff collars; underneath, Angie rummaging now to make sure, a black bib, a black suit, and a breviary. The man was a priest.

Angie spread the coat and tucked it in, trying to cover what he had not ought to have seen. He wanted to laugh and cry at once, and he heard the funny little sounds coming out of himself while he took out the money which he had by then put in his wallet and stuffed it under the coat.

He was at the escalator before he realized he had put his own eight dollars in as well. He was left with only the change in his pocket. But he did not go back.

7 Marks spent the early afternoon going over some new evidence in an old case. It had been a homicidal summer in New York. By two-thirty a trickle of information on the Grossman case had begun to come in, a measurement of the knife, the fact that it had a hilt similar to those of hunting knives although the blade was narrower than usual; shreds of dark blue wool in the cat's claws . . . Grossman had been wearing a sweater vest, the wool in which matched that found in the cat's claws. No time discrepancy in Ruggio's story could be proven conclusively from the blood stains on his shoes. A heel print in a blood splotch on the floor, however, did suggest that Ruggio might have been on the scene at separate times. It gave Marks something with which to confront the man.

Marks arrived back at the precinct house to be handed the necessary papers admitting him to Grossman's safety deposit box in the Essex Street Bank. He decided to walk the few blocks distance, for it was a walk Grossman might have taken himself. On the East side of the Bowery he would have been a Jew among Jews. And Puerto Ricans, Marks soon realized. The neighborhood was changing fast. Most of the merchants were Jewish, but their chief custom no longer was. Once Marks had loved to come down here with his grandfather. In those days he would have preferred to be a ghetto boy. He had liked the gusto and the anger, the quick passion and the grumbling loyalty of the streets, pushcart politics, the quivering beards of the men who argued outside the office of the *Daily Forward*. If Grossman had turned his back on the ghetto of his own people, why? As long as he was going into a ghetto. Anger because America had spared its Jews his ordeal? But he had come through. At what price? That was the question. Sour and hostile, warming only occasionally to the likes of a Julie Borghese. Why among Italians, and "in" religious articles? Tomasino was trying to coax the source of the violinist story out of the *Post* reporter. The inspector would say that Marks was starting too far back in the man's life, that it was sheer romanticism. And it probably was. Otherwise, he would have stepped out as fast as he stepped into the case.

In the bank, one of the last of those basilica-like structures with a domed ceiling and marble pillars, Marks followed a mini-skirted clerk to the desk of the vault custodian. Mr. Krakauer was a slightly stooped man, near the age for retirement, and Marks had the feeling that when he went he would take his desk plaque with him. He settled the detective in a private, air-conditioned room whose one decoration was a picture of Theodore Roosevelt. When Krakauer brought the small narrow box, Marks asked him if he remembered Grossman.

"Oh, yes. I remember him. I was kept at attention every time until he took inventory."

"I'm going to ask you to do the same thing," Marks said.

"You, I can understand, a witness."

Marks noted three bankbooks showing consecutive deposits, in the Essex, no withdrawals, the ownership papers to the building on Hester Street, tax receipts, and a document of United States citizenship. "Would you say there is anything missing from what you have seen in the past?" Marks asked as he gave the pen to Krakauer.

"I wouldn't know about one or two of those tax receipts, if they were missing. But I'd say you've got the works, lieutenant."

Marks sat without looking at anything for a minute after the custodian left him. The fact that the bankbooks were here, not at home in the desk or upstairs, or in the safe, was a story in itself. Grossman's private life, such as there was of it in

America, was spread on the table in front of the detective. The shop was a sham, the safe somebody else's, and the second-floor apartment a hole in which he hid himself every night. Possibly from himself.

Marks took up the record of savings first. The account had been opened in 1966 with a deposit of $2,900 in cash. The monthly deposits since, with accumulating interest, totaled $56,472.

The deed to the building on Hester Street: Grossman had bought it from the Ambrose Corporation the same year. This particularly interested Marks because Alberto Ruggio worked for that outfit. Grossman had bought the property from them for $46,000, an amount conveyed to the company on Gross-man's behalf, by his attorney, Frank Gerosa of Weehawken, New Jersey, who was licensed to practice in New York as well.

A brief study of the tax receipts showed that the property had been re-evaluated to a much higher worth three years before. It made for quite a hike in Grossman's taxes. Marks checked the withdrawals in the bankbooks: none, even at tax dates. Nor did the deposits diminish at those times. The increase was passed on to either his customers or his employers; possibly to both.

With a reluctance that could only have to do with Grossman's having been a concentration camp Jew, Marks opened the citizenship papers. Benjamin Grossman had been born in Berlin on April 19, 1906. He had entered the United States at the port of New York in 1946. His sponsors were Anna and Frank Gerosa.

Marks used the bank telephone to check out Gerosa with the Bar Association. He was still in practice, and his record was clean. The bank manager arranged to have the contents of Grossman's box xeroxed. Marks addressed the envelope himself for the messenger. He wanted a man named Wescott, an imaginative detective, to work on the background of the Ambrose Corporation.

By the time he got back to the stationhouse, the information had come through that according to his number Grossman had been an internee of Buchenwald.

Marks called Gerosa's office in Weehawken. The lawyer was out, but expected back in the late afternoon.

Tomasino had traced the violinist story to one of the warehousemen at the Ambrose Corporation. The reporter who had picked it up first had been trying for something extra from Ruggio.

"Let's try that ourselves," Marks said. "On our way to Weehawken."

"Weehawken," Tomasino repeated. "Now that's a country I've always wanted to visit."

Marks liked Tomasino, a self-assured, chunky young man of twenty-four with long sideburns and as modern a cut to his clothes as regulations would allow. All Marks actually knew of him was that he had grown up in Little Italy and that he was engaged to be married. He was very, very young to have made detective-first-grade, and Marks availed himself of the jammed traffic in the narrow streets to find out how it had come about.

Tomasino was the son of a tailor. He had gone from Cathedral High School to New York University for a year and then to the Police Academy. After starting as a patrolman in his own neighborhood, he was promoted to detective under Regan. But when Regan went back to uniform, Tomasino had asked for Homicide and got it.

"What got you out of uniform in the first place?" Marks asked.

"Luck and a little pull."

"Tell me about the luck."

"My partner and I interrupted a jewel heist on Canal Street. I spotted the getaway car and commandeered a cab when they took off, seeing us. My partner stayed on the scene. The cab had a two-way radio. That was the luck. We caught the lot of them."

"I remember," Marks said.

"Big deal," Tomasino said with a shy grin.

A din of truck horns started, as though the drivers could

blast their way out of the jam with noise. Marks waited until that wave of passion subsided. "If you had to pick an angle on Grossman, what would you say, Tommy?"

"Heroin."

"Mob controlled?"

"Controlled by someone outside," the young detective said carefully.

"By outside, what do you mean?"

"Outside the neighborhood."

"Do you think Grossman had anything to say about the control?"

"I got a feeling, no. But he'd have known something. Too much maybe."

"What are you going on, Tommy?"

Tomasino shrugged and the color came up in his cheeks.

"He was a smart Jew?"

"I guess that went through my mind. I got my pride too."

Marks gave a grunt of amusement. "Look, Tommy, shit is shit. Right?"

"Right."

"Now that we got that straight, I'll tell you what came out of the bank vault."

"Ambrose Corporation," Tomasino repeated. "They're supposed to be clean, lieutenant."

"So are the police, but if Grossman was in narcotics, there'd just about have to be a pay-off, wouldn't you agree?"

Marks interpreted the noise Tomasino made as his trying to say yes and no at the same time.

"But you don't want to start the flack."

"I don't want to lead a scalping party, that's the truth, Dave, which doesn't mean I know anything. And Grossman's death, the way he died—that's not the way the mob would do it . . . I don't think."

Marks had to agree with him. "Unless they imported international talent."

"I got the Immigration Bureau started on Ruggio if that's what you mean."

"Good man," Marks said.

The warning light came up on the car temperature gauge just as the traffic began to move. The jam, as it turned out, had originated at the dock of the Ambrose warehouse. Marks and Tomasino drove up in time to see a tall, burly fellow with a heavy blue jaw getting dressed down by a man twice his age and half his size.

"That's Ruggio," Tomasino said. "According to the boss, he doesn't know his left hand from his right."

"He looks like somebody they'd have brought over in the old days to put in the fight game."

"Three heads," Tomasino said, holding up his fists, "and not a brain in any of them."

Marks parked too close to a fire plug but it was the only available space. He watched the big awkward man who made his only defense in gestures. "Let's see what the personnel office has on him first, shall we? It'll give us a chance to look over the premises."

They walked through a huge arched warehouse that reminded Marks of a theater.

"I'm not sure it wasn't," Tomasino said. "Maybe a hundred years ago. There's one in here somewhere."

They passed stacked wheels of Romano cheese, cases of stringed provolone, sausages coiled like snakes in straw baskets giving off a fragrance tinged with garlic. The deeper they got into the building, the cooler it was.

The offices were air-conditioned. Marks asked the personnel manager, whose name was Lavia, if they could see the employment record of Alberto Ruggio.

"What's the poor bastard done now?"

"Just call it a character reference," Marks said. He made a perfunctory show of identification.

Lavia beckoned to a stenographer with his forefinger. "Ruggio, Alberto."

"What's your hiring procedure where immigrants are concerned?"

"Work permit, social security number—we're glad to get

immigrants if they speak Italian. We don't claim to be an equal opportunity employer, lieutenant, but to our own, we're a lot fairer than those who are."

Marks thought that over and avoided looking at Tomasino. When the file card came, he took out his pen, intending to note the vital statistics, birthplace, age, and so forth.

"I got a better idea," Lavia said. "Why don't I have the girl make you out a duplicate card?"

The stenographer plucked the card out of his hand without waiting further instruction. She sashayed back to her typewriter. He might wiggle his finger at her, but the wiggle of her backside was a more eloquent impertinence.

"No references?" Marks observed when the card was given to him.

"No, sir. With our firm the only reference a man needs is his day's work."

When they got back to the loading zone, another truck was backing in, the foreman himself directing the driver. Ruggio was not in sight. They waited a couple of minutes, Marks watching his time: he did not want to get caught in the height of the tunnel traffic to New Jersey. Finally he asked the foreman where the big fellow had gone.

"He's walked off the job for all I know, and I care less. He ought to be herding sheep."

Marks swore to himself as they went back to the car.

"He'll turn up home," Tomasino said. "And with the wife and kid to support, he'll be back on the job tomorrow."

"I took something for granted, Tommy, and I don't like it."

"What?"

"That you can judge a man by his looks."

They took the time to double back to Hester Street. The officer on duty outside the building assured them that Ruggio had not come home.

8 They heard Gerosa's laughter before they reached the smoked-glass door of his office. Frank Gerosa, Attorney at Law: a one-man practice in a building that might well qualify among the historic landmarks of Weehawken. His curly white hair, faintly yellowed with the sun, and his bronzed brow proclaimed him the outdoors type, and his camaraderie with his tidy, middle-aged secretary suggested a loquacious, call-me-Frank exterior. He pegged Marks and Tomasino the minute they walked in the door. "Gentlemen. Manhattan Squad . . . what?"

A short time later he slipped as lithely into his reminiscences of Grossman. "I had no use for the man before I ever saw him, and when I did see him . . ." He flung his hand out, a gesture of distaste. "A debt of honor is all right, but you don't want to be spat on for paying it. He had saved a life in our family—my wife's youngest brother, Anthony, who, it turned out, was a communist partisan. Anyway, before he could save him, he'd had to save himself, and considering his racial origins, that was more than, well, say a lawyer could have done for him. So if he's dead—and I'll take your word for that—you got to figure he's twenty-five, thirty years up on the game."

"The game?" Marks was perfectly aware of his meaning, but he wasn't taken with Gerosa. He hated having to dig for a man under the gloss. Also, the golf trophies all over the office were highly polished, the law books dusty. The place was full of chairs and ashtrays, like a clubroom. He practiced by rote and politics. But then, many lawyers did.

"All right, lieutenant. There's a lot of serious things I call a game. I'm not a solemn man. What I'm saying is, he was half a lifetime up on most of the other inmates of Auschwitz."

Auschwitz. Grossman's number identified him as having been interned in Buchenwald. Marks said: "Auschwitz in 1945—a German Jew in that camp had to be pretty rare."

"One in a million," Gerosa said, apparently missing a point that Marks did not press. "He was an arrogant bastard. But he saved Anthony's life, and he did not hesitate to come to America to collect."

"To collect what?"

"A life for a life, shall we say? That's old testament, isn't it?"

Marks felt his temper quicken. "Let's skip the scripture and keep to the facts, shall we, sir?"

The lawyer smiled. It too was rote with him, getting under a man's skin. Marks again felt his own judgment off in this interrogation. Gerosa was saying, "I myself prefer facts, but I don't have many to offer. Will you have a drink, boys?" He swung round in his chair and opened a panel to an inset liquor cabinet. Marks thought instantly of the safe in Grossman's shop. The buildings would be of an age. "My one modern accommodation, which would be impossible in the paper-thin walls they put up today."

"A beer if you have one, please," Marks said. He wanted to cool off in more ways than one. "How about you, Tommy?"

"That would go down good."

Gerosa closed the cabinet and went to the water cooler. He brought three cans from the ice and opened them. "Tomasino —a jewel heist, right?"

The young detective nodded, the color rising to his face.

Gerosa knew about that, Marks thought, yet he claimed not to have heard of Grossman's death until now.

The lawyer took a long drink and belched behind his hand. "The facts: I've said Tony was a communist, a political prisoner. When the war was over, he wrote and said his life had been saved by a man named Grossman. Since he could not come to America himself—which was Anna, my wife's dream of course, but with the politics he was persona non grata—he

66

wanted us to sponsor Grossman when he arrived. Now it is interesting, and I think you would call it a fact, Lieutenant Marks, how Grossman happened to save his life. As a kid, Tony learned the flute. He'd played for the Milano Opera. To find that out, Grossman would have had to have some kind of liberty—wouldn't you say? That's guesswork, not fact. But he got Tony into an orchestra. An orchestra in Auschwitz: how do you like that, lieutenant?"

Marks was more upset than he had any intention of showing: "Where's your brother-in-law today, Mr. Gerosa?"

"Five years dead in an Italian grave. He died of cancer, not of the Boche."

"Could Grossman speak English when he arrived?"

"He could get by. Look, I'm not trying to bait you, lieutenant. I'm an easy-going, friendly guy, but I could see the chip on your shoulder the minute you came in the office."

Marks turned to Tomasino. "Why the hell didn't you brush it off?"

They all laughed and the inverview went easier after that.

"Let us say we are both a little uptight: that is a word I learned from my grandchildren. They don't use it anymore, but I'm stuck with it. You see, in those days we Italian Americans were pretty defensive. A lot of us had been proud of Il Duce before the war. What did we know? In Italy the trains ran on time. I don't think they have since, by the way. Then they hung him upside down and some of us felt that way too. Upside down. So, when this arrogant gentleman arrives with the air of doing us a favor, our hospitality did not run over. I gave him the works myself—he should look for work in the needle trades, in the garment section, or maybe a Jewish delicatessen, the whole *schmeer*. I had friends, contacts, some of my best friends, etcetera. But Mr. Grossman would go out in the morning in sartorial splendor and come home at night unemployed. There was not a job good enough for him. At least, that's what I thought then that it was all about. Afterwards, I wondered if he hadn't been steering clear of the Jews."

"Afraid of them?" It had, of course, gone through Marks' mind, too: had others died so that he could live?

"Something like that."

"Did he live with you for long?"

"For several weeks. The children were scared of him. He used to watch them, staring at them. When they saw him they'd run away and he'd scream after them, "Run, run!""

Gerosa finished his beer and went on: "I used to say to myself, I wouldn't want his dreams. But the funny thing was, I used to have his dreams. When you live with somebody and you see things in the paper, you take them in with your guts, where if he wasn't there, you'd hardly even have noticed them. You know what I mean?"

Marks nodded. It was the American experience—unless you were a Jew.

Gerosa sat thinking and Marks left him to it. Tomasino offered a cigarette. The lieutenant accepted. Gerosa came to life and lit their cigarettes with a desk lighter. He stared at the flame until it flickered out of its own accord. "I owe that man something, son of a bitch or not."

"What?"

"It's a four-dollar word—integrity. How do you like that?" He got up and paced the room, repeating to himself, "How do you like that?" Suddenly he swung around on Tomasino. "How do you get ahead on the police force, a young wop like you? Your father makes suits."

"Maybe that helps me get ahead on the police force," Tomasino said. The color rose to his face again.

"How do you get ahead as a lawyer?" Gerosa went on, forgetting about Tomasino. "You scratch my back, I'll scratch yours. Only if you're Italian, you got to watch whose back you're scratching. A law education doesn't come cheap. I could have made money, a lot of money. The law is above the law, you know. In those days, maybe I wasn't hungry, but I was no fat cat either. I looked at Grossman and I said to myself, it isn't worth it. Nothing is worth it. Sooner or later you got to face yourself. You know what truth is, gentlemen? Truth is self-justification. That is everybody's truth, but that is not God's truth. I thought I was telling God's truth. Well, I have no regrets. That's not right either: I have one: I prosecuted Grossman, I convicted him, and I would have sentenced him. I tried. What I was really doing, I was taking out on him my anger at my own people. I had to fight their money, the gangster money, the Family money. They had plenty for smart lawyers, and I was a smart lawyer. I had to fight them and I had to fight myself. So why don't I feel good about what I'm telling you? Grossman was a shit, I have said it, but without him, maybe I wouldn't have made it. He was a coward who wanted to live when I thought he should have wanted to die. Do you know what I did to him? I made him fiddle at my daughter's christening. So much righteousness at a time like that. I got him a violin, and I said, Play!"

"Did he?"

"He played. And the sweat poured off him. Green sweat. Ever seen it?"

"A time or two. I've even felt it."

Gerosa sat down again and wiped his face. He looked at the handkerchief as though expecting color to his own sweat.

"What else about Grossman? Where did he go and why?"

"Well, he played at a wedding now and then, people who got onto him at our party. It was a grandiose affair. You know us Italians. People talk about Victoria's christening to this day. Then one day, when there was nobody in the house but him, he packed up and left. He left the violin on the cot he'd been sleeping on in the attic, only he'd put his foot through its belly. Some smart psychiatrist would tell you it was better than what he could've left us up there. I found out from a neighbor that he'd got a job on your side of the river. Before I heard from him direct, he was ready to become a citizen and he wanted me to be present. He wanted to pay a debt. He did: for the violin, and my legal fee, and you know what he said about the rest? 'I assume the hospitality was on the house.' How do you like that?"

69

"I rather like it," Marks said. "Tell me, Mr. Gerosa, is the Ambrose Corporation 'Family' oriented?"

"If I knew, do you think I'd be fool enough to tell you?"

"I'd consider it confidential."

"I'd consider it suicidal."

"Why do you think he retained you to close the property deal?"

"Because I was the one honest lawyer he could be sure of."

"But surely, Gerosa, there was something wrong with the deal: forty-six thousand dollars for a chunk of Manhattan?"

Gerosa looked at Marks mournfully. "Would you say today, lieutenant, that he got a bargain?"

An artful dodger. Marks glanced at his partner: "Any questions, Tommy?"

"I was wondering, Mr. Gerosa: did you tell his story around—say at the christening party, the concentration camp part?"

"I don't remember to who, but I didn't make any secret of it, not in my frame of mind in those days."

"So he could 've been blackmailed? Say somebody's relatives died because of him."

"If I were in your shoes, I'd consider the possibility."

Marks felt a rankle at the smugness, which he smothered. He got up. "Was he a good violinist?"

"We thought he was. We used to call him Rubenoff and his violin. Do you remember on the radio?"

Neither detective did.

"I'm getting old," Gerosa said.

Marks was a long time silent on the way back to the city. He was thinking of blackmail, reprisal . . . He thought again of the square of clean glass at the height of a woman's face.

"It was like a history lesson back there," Tomasino said, "Mussolini and all that."

Which turned Marks' thinking back to something else. "Remember in Miss Borghese's statement this morning, Gross-

70

man's calling the teen-agers baby fascists: do they fit in this picture as you see it, Tommy?"

"I don't know. What I thought—there's a lot of clubs in the area, the kids making like their old men. Which I don't mean makes any of them fascists. What's a fascist? A left-wing name for patriotism? Our kids are pretty strong on that. We Italian-Americans take a lot of crap these days." The young man lapsed into silence.

Perhaps he had thought of Gerosa's integrity. Marks probed, "You did notice the swastikas in the hallway?"

"Yes, sir, and there's something else I noticed: Grossman's is the only shop in the block without a flag in the window. I mean even an American flag. You wouldn't think it would make any difference to him. Go along with the kids, right?"

"I'm missing something in there. How does it connect with the kids?"

"They went around with the flags. They got people to close up shop on Italian American Day. Two thousand people turned out from Little Italy alone."

"I wonder if Grossman closed up."

"I can find out."

"I'd like to get acquainted myself in the neighborhood, Tommy. I'll buy you dinner. Then let's look in on some of the youngsters' clubs."

"Tonight?"

"That's what I had in mind."

"Don't you have a family, Dave?"

"I moved out years ago—it's made for a very good relationship."

"Don't you ever think about getting married?"

"Sometimes. My mother thinks of it oftener, my getting married."

"Same here. I hardly knew I proposed to the girl when the women set the date."

"The folks want grandchildren," Marks said. "That's what it's all about."

"Mine already got seven."

"Then maybe it's not what it's all about," Marks said.

He stopped at Hester Street, and when he learned that Ruggio had not come home by his regular hour, Marks fed the information on the Ambrose employment form through Center Street for verification from the appropriate government sources.

9 Angie's imagination played tricks on him all afternoon. Everywhere he rested, people seemed to be looking at him. Every time he passed a cop and looked back at him, the cop was also looking back at him. He would get a number of things straightened out in his mind, a sequence of events, say, that proved he had nothing to do with the murder, and the whole thing would fall apart. He thought he could forget about the coat, Alice—he didn't think she would go volunteering what she'd done about the plane ticket to the police—and even that the man was a priest. Up to this point his reasoning soothed him. Then Ric moved into the picture with his attitude of owning Angie. It was as though the whole ordeal, the whole Killing Eye ritual had been made up as the perfect trap for Mr. Grossman and Angie Palermo. If he did get questioned about the murder, Angie realized, he was going to have to tell about stealing the coat. He wouldn't say the man was a priest, but he'd have to tell the rest to prove where he was from eleven o'clock on.

He sat a long part of the afternoon in Washington Square, watching the summer students come and go with their books. He had almost flunked out of junior high, and yet he had a high I.Q. His happiest distraction was the singing of the young people in the park and the way they made love to their guitars, and that brought him back to Alice . . . only last night, a century and a half ago.

By suppertime he knew he had to go home and the sooner the better. He didn't think his mother would go to the police looking for him, but you could never tell with her what she

73

would do. He could never guess it right. A clout or a kiss: he just wouldn't know till he got there. She was bound to have put the whole neighborhood on the lookout for him.

He listened at the door before he put the key into the lock. There was a tingling kind of stillness to the whole building. At any minute the doors would burst open, a population explosion. Now every family was in the kitchen at the back, the only things in the hallway, empty baby carriages and the smell of the pasta sauce. He heard voices in his own apartment, which started the pulse drumming in his head again. Then he heard his mother's laughter climb the scale. It gave him relief, then hurt, then anger, an instant-mix of feelings which made him wish again for the plane ticket.

He opened the door to silence and then called out as though he didn't know, "Anybody home?"

More silence. They had heard the key, her and Mr. Rotelli. He was sure that's who was with his mother. There was a light under the kitchen door. He imagined them looking at one another, his mother rolling her knowing eyes toward the door. The smell of oregano sweetened the house. He lit the floor lamp. The *New York Post* lay beside the chair where Mr. Rotelli had dropped it, page by page. He could get away with it, not Angie. Angie wanted to look in the paper to see if there was anything new, but there wasn't time. His mother pushed open the kitchen door and switched on the light over the dining room table. Nobody ever ate at the table, and the bowl of fruit which sparkled under the light was made of glass. She didn't say anything, just waited. Angie calculated that if the police had been there it would be different, and she'd not have been laughing.

"Hello, mama."

"Good *morning*, Angelo." The false smile he hated reinforced the sarcasm.

"Did you worry about me?"

"No. I don't worry about you no more. I don't worry about your brother. I worry about me, nobody else."

Angie approached her cautiously. "I'm hungry, mama." It

wasn't so, but his appetite had got him out of scrapes before. She wanted him to eat, to get some shape to him.

"Ha! You were right, Mr. Rotelli,"—this over her shoulder to the man in the kitchen—"His heart is in his belly. That's how he remembered his mother."

Angie edged toward the door. He didn't think she would strike him in front of Mr. Rotelli, and if she did, he'd use his father's words, the ones he'd been holding back for years. But she did not raise a hand. She moved out of the doorway and let him pass. He caught the scent of perfume, and just for a second wished she would grab his head as she used to and hold it against her bosom. That wasn't going to happen with Mr. Rotelli around.

"Good evening, Mr. Rotelli."

The table was set for two, Rotelli sitting in Angie's place. Angie sat down opposite him.

"Mr. Palermo," Rotelli said solemnly, making a little mock formal bow. He took a cigarette from a silver case and tapped it on the case. He was a smaller man than Angie remembered his own father, but with the large mustache, a thick head of carefully combed hair, and long sideburns he looked up to date and very sure of himself. He made a big thing of his hands: the way he used them put Angie in mind of dancers. The nails shone. They were probably polished, him being a hair dresser in a hotel shop where there was a manicurist.

Angie's mother stood, her hands on her hips. "Angelo, are you in trouble?"

"No," he said, as though the idea was ridiculous.

"That's what you think," she exploded. "Let me tell you, you are making one big mistake. I got everybody in the neighborhood looking for you, everybody feels sorry for your mother. But Angelo is such a good boy, they say, something must have happened to him. The good ones, the quiet ones, they get beat up, they get the knife in the back. Everybody's got a knife if they don't have a gun. Mr. Rotelli's got a gun. What good will it do him? . . ." She ranted on, less and less sensible as she let the anger out. What about? It wasn't all about him, Angie felt. If she had been all that scared on his account, she wouldn't have been laughing before she knew that he'd come home.

Angie glanced at Rotelli and caught a smile under the mustache. Angie felt he knew then: she was mad—since he was safe—that he'd come home when he did. She'd been all set for an evening with Mr. Rotelli: the flowered napkins and the silver forks, even if it was the kitchen table. There was a big fan in the kitchen window. The gold-stemmed wine glasses from Murano were out, and only two places set, not three in case the prodigal son came home.

To hell with both of them, Angie decided. His eyes took in the wine bottle, something special Mr. Rotelli had brought. The man's eyes followed his. Rotelli reached out his graceful hand to the bottle and poured wine into his and Angie's glasses. His mother was raving on now about the nice boys she thought he had taken up with. She was talking about the Little Brothers and Angie tried to listen, to get some sense out of what she was saying: she'd gone to the clubhouse on the way home from work. Nobody would tell her anything but she could feel they all knew something, all of them so mysterious. Mr. Rotelli touched his wine glass to Angie's making a little bell-like tinkle. It shut off the flow of his mother's words. Rotelli winked at the boy.

His mother struck his arm when Angie reached for the glass. "Not a drop until you tell me."

"Katerina," Rotelli said softly, "you have not given him a chance to tell us anything."

Us. Angie had heard it.

His mother waited, her arms folded. She was wearing a dress he had not seen before, a misty red dress that you could see her slip through and the shape of her big breasts.

"I was with a woman," he said. He had intended to say a girl friend, but changed his mind at the last minute, wanting to make sure she got the point, smack, like a slap in the face.

It worked. He could almost hear shock in her breathing. Her

face puckered up as though she was going to cry. She pulled out the chair and sat down.

"So," Mr. Rotelli said, "a boy goes out of the house one day, and a man comes back the next. Congratulations."

If looks could have killed, Angie would not have had to worry about Mr. Rotelli anymore.

His mother laid her hand on Angie's on the table. "Why?" she said, and there were real tears in her eyes.

Rotelli threw up his hands. "He's a man, that's why! Let me tell you, you can thank God, the way things are in the world today, it was a woman."

"You shut up," his mother said. She turned back to Angie. "An older woman. She picked you up."

Angie pulled his hand out from beneath his mother's. "She's not that old."

Rotelli gave a bark of laughter.

Angie wished he had never said the thing in the first place. "She's a very nice person. We went . . . to the Palisades Amusement Park."

"In my day," Rotelli said, "it was Coney Island. Under the Board Walk."

"Is she Italian? Do I know her? Where did you meet her? On the street? Tell the truth, Angelo."

Angie got the feeling that all of them were talking to themselves. Even he was. "She's not a prostitute," he said.

"You will go to a doctor the first thing in the morning."

"Jesus Christ!" Rotelli exploded, and pushed away from the table. He got to his feet. "You are a crazy woman, Katerina, and I am beginning to understand. I'm going home."

"Sit down and explain to me why it is crazy that I worry about my own son?"

"How can I explain? You can explain to an ear, but not to a tongue. Do you know what the trouble is, Katerina? I can explain to you in one word: Irish priests. Two words. In Italy when a boy turns into a man, everybody knows he would go to a goat or a bishop, but better a woman. And the young people today all over the world, they go to one another and they say, Let's make love, not war, and I say God bless them and to hell with the priests."

Angie sat stunned. He had not known Mr. Rotelli was like that at all. Now he didn't know what to make of him. He took a sip of the wine. He liked it a lot better than Alice's. The sweet stuff turned his stomach.

Rotelli set his cigarette on the crimson ashtray, and went behind Angie's mother. He put his hands on her shoulders and gently rubbed the back of her neck with his thumbs. She was always complaining of how much it hurt there. "Katerina, my dove, you cannot have it both ways. You want him to grow up and stop dreaming. The next minute you sing him a lullaby."

"He is a dreamer," she said, but she closed her eyes and let her head loll back.

"So, Angelo, what do you dream of? What do you want to be besides a great lover?" Rotelli said.

Angie hesitated, and then took the cunning plunge his instinct prompted. "One of the things, I'd like to be a dancer."

"A dancer?" the man repeated thoughtfully.

"Sometimes I think of it, the way you use your hands, you know?"

Rotelli looked at his hands and turned them round and round slowly. "I have always been very proud of my hands," he said.

"Don't stop," Angie's mother said, but of the massage. "Last week he wanted to be a priest."

Not last week, Angie thought. That's when he had started thinking about Mr. Grossman. The sick, hopeless feeling came over him again.

"I have a customer," Mr. Rotelli was saying, "a big *macher* on Broadway. He won't let anybody dress his hair except Rotelli. Or trim his beard. I will speak to him."

"What kind of a job is it to be a dancer? In Sicily the gipsies dance for money." His mother straightened up and opened her eyes. "Do you want to be a gipsy?"

Angie thought he would love it, but he did not say so.

Rotelli said, "What I'm afraid is, it is already too late for you. I have heard him say dancers must start before they are twelve years old."

"I always dance when I'm alone," Angie said.

"How can you dance alone?" his mother said.

"That's the kind of dancer I want to be." His spirits were coming up again. He had not really done anything wrong. Not anything terribly wrong. "Mr. Rotelli?"

"We'll see, we'll see," Rotelli drew back the cuff of his silk suit and looked at his watch. "It is almost eight o'clock, Katerina."

"I'll put the light under the water. The salad is ready."

Rotelli sat down and sipped his wine, his eyes humorous as he explored Angie's face over the rim of the glass. Angie knew he was looking at him. He did not meet his eyes. As though reading his mind, the man said, "So Rotelli is not the worst guy in the world after all?"

Angie gave a shake of his head and grinned.

"Get a knife and fork and a place for yourself, my little dancer," his mother said, "and somebody pour me a glass of wine."

Angie did not feel hungry in spite of the fact that he had not eaten since the fancy breakfast with Alice. "Mama, I didn't tell you the truth. I had something to eat before I came home."

"What does she do, this lady friend of yours?"

"She works in a restaurant."

"So you will eat," Rotelli said. "But not too much if you want to be a dancer. Meat and salad. Forget the bread and the pasta."

"His mother's a baker and you tell him to forget the bread."

Angie wanted to ask Mr. Rotelli about his friend, the one he was going to speak to, but before he got the chance, the phone rang, and Angie was sure just from the way it rang that it was for him. It might even be the police.

"It's probably for me," Angie said, before his mother could get to the door. The phone was in the dining room.

Rotelli laughed. "Look at his face, as pale as a turtle dove."

Angie prayed and let the door swing closed behind him. If it was the police they would come to the house. "Hello?" He could hardly hear his own voice.

"You better come right over to the clubhouse, Angie."

"Ric?"

The phone went to a buzz, but Angie knew it was Ric. He put the phone back in its cradle and watched the moisture disappear from where he had held it in his hand. He was sure it was Ric. He didn't know how he felt about facing the Little Brothers. If only the police had arrested somebody by now, Angie Palermo would be a hero in the club. But if Angie Palermo was going to be a hero, Ric Bonelli would not be calling him to come to the meeting that way. He pushed open the door a few inches and said, "It was for me. I'll see you later, mama. Thank you, Mr. Rotelli."

"Where are you going?"

"To my club, mama."

"You come home to your own bed tonight, Angelo, or else don't you come home at all no more. Hear me?"

"Come to my house," Rotelli said. "Want a key?"

Angie did not answer. A joke. And he didn't want any more keys. He was feeling sickish again. In the bathroom he put cold water on his face and that helped. Then he was chilled again. He went to his room and put on a sweater. He longed to crawl into his own bed and start a whole new dream . . . but he knew he could not do that. He heard them talking in the kitchen as he went out. He could not remember if he had thanked Mr. Rotelli. But what difference did it make, considering the other things that could happen to him?

There was no sign of Ric on the street, only swarms of kids and women who told him his mother had been looking all day for him. He cut through a lot where the demolition ball and bulldozers had carved a canyon between buildings. A line of wash hung high overhead, all pink in the last of the sunset. A gust of wind puffed out the man's shirts. He stood a few seconds in the middle of the lot. He heard a loud bang, a firecracker or a backfire, then a motorcycle warming up to a roar. For a minute he lost himself in a childhood game: an army of riders bore down on him and he had to find cover before they could spray him with machinegun bullets. He made for the Ukrainian church on the next corner. The fantasy faded when he saw the priest close the gates and go inside. He remembered how, when he was six or seven, he ran with the big kids while they taunted the bearded priest. He'd come out flying after them like Bat Man, his arms flailing. There was choir practice going on in the church as Angie passed under the windows, men's voices chanting, a lisping, whispering sound mixed in with the foreign words. Angie brought the sound down in his mind to "sworry," then, "sorry."

He repeated the one word over and over to himself, a prayer of sorts, until he reached the stoop under which was the entrance to the Little Brothers' clubroom. It had once belonged to a group of men, but the sign still served: MEMBERS ONLY. His three slow raps on the door committed him to enter.

Pete the Turk opened the door to him and went back to the table where the five members of the council sat in the same places Angie remembered them sitting the night he took the oaths. Only they looked at him differently: Angie had the feeling they were as scared of him as he was of them, and it struck him that they thought he had actually killed Grossman.

Louis said, "Come over to the light, Angie."

There was only the one light in the room. It hung over the table. Angie approached. He tried to look at Louis but he had glanced at the light bulb and the glare bleared his vision.

"On your oath, Palermo, did you kill Grossman with your own hand?"

"I did not."

"When did you last see him?"

Angie said a crazy thing: it came out of all the interrogations he had watched on television: "Alive?"

"Did you see him dead?" Louis asked, quick as a shot.

"No. I don't know why I said that. I mean, I saw him about eleven o'clock. He climbed up on that platform in the window and looked back at me. I . . . went away then."

"Do you know who killed him?"

Angie glanced at Ric. He couldn't help it. Then he looked down. "No."

"What'd you look at me for?" Ric said in a high pitch.

Angie didn't answer.

"Angie?" Louis demanded.

"I was thinking about Ric calling me to come here."

"I didn't call you. Tonight, you mean?"

"Twenty minutes ago."

"I was here by then, wasn't I, captain?"

"All right, a half hour maybe," Angie said.

"I swear by my oath as a Little Brother . . ."

Louis silenced him by a thump of his hand on the table. "Before you got the phone call, Angie, didn't you intend to come here?"

Angie shook his head. He tried to think what might come next.

"Why not?"

"I thought the police might be following me. I mean if somebody'd seen me hanging around Grossman's so much."

"You are a good Brother," Louis said. "Sit down."

The captain made room for him between himself and Pete. There was a backless chair a few feet away. Angie chose that rather than wrestle with one of the folding chairs that stood against the wall. He brought it. Before he sat down, Louis pulled the chair even closer to the table than Angie had placed it.

"Do you think it could 've been a cop who phoned you—like he wanted to see what you'd do?"

Angie shook his head. "It was Ric."

"I swear . . ." Ric shouted.

"Shut up, Ric." To Angie, Louis said: "It *sounded* like Ric. Okay?"

"Okay," he said, but he knew that voice better than any in the world.

"Now tell us what you found out about Grossman."

Angie told everything he could remember: the abuse of the cat, the payoff to the policeman, the black man whom he had seen twice. "The way he came into the hall after me, it was like he knew the place inside and out. He could have been the one . . ."

Louis interrupted. "Forget that. Do you know what was going on?"

"I know what I think was going on," Angie said. "Drugs. I think there must be heroin or something in the little statues."

There was silence, absolute, noncommittal silence, but every Brother's eyes were on him.

"Now let's get back to the phone call tonight, the voice that sounded like Ric's. What did he say to you?"

"I don't know—all he said was, you better come to the clubhouse, Angie. Something like that. And when I said Ric?, whoever it was hung up."

This time Ric kept his mouth shut.

Louis did all the talking. "There was a lot of money in a safe in the back of the shop. A cop I know says eighty thousand bucks. That's the big league. And if they thought there was any chance of little guys like us spilling anything to the cops, we'd be in real trouble. Do you know what I'm talking about, Angie?"

"I'm not sure."

"It could be a mob operation. What they call the Mafia."

"I see," Angie said, but he did not see at all. He did not believe there was a Mafia, not in the 1970s. Once there had been. Now there might be Families linked by blood protecting themselves, in business together, yes. And maybe there were crime syndicates, but not Italian. That was a smear, propaganda meant to disgrace the Italian-Americans and to cover up secret operations of the FBI. But Louis had just spoken of the Mafia, and Angie plainly remembered that the Little Brothers had picketed the FBI headquarters. He remembered their sign: MAFIA? PROVE IT!

"But Grossman was a Jew," he said.

"And the pusher black," Louis said.

Angie thought he understood a little better. There *was* a Mafia, but it wasn't all Italian.

Louis said: "We've got to have some facts from you, Ric: what started you on Grossman?"

Angie realized that he'd been right: Ric was at the bottom of whatever trouble he was in.

"Just keeping my eyes open," Ric said. "Like all of yous . . . we all agreed, didn't we?"

"Be specific. We may be up against something and we got to know."

"I seen this guy," Ric said, "this black guy drop one of them little statues on the street. It broke and he went crazy trying to sweep it up. The Jew ran out with a broom and some paper, sweeping up the white stuff. And when a patrol car drove up, Grossman bowed and waved at them and the cops didn't even stop. So I figured—who wouldn't?"

Angie could not tell whether the other Brothers believed Ric or not. He didn't himself. Something was wrong, and yet . . .

"Describe the black man," Louis said.

Angie had not described him, he realized, and Louis would call on him next. He was going to have to stand up to Ric.

"I didn't see him real close," Ric started.

But he was not going to have to finish: someone was pounding on the door who meant it. They were coming in. The Little Brothers froze in their seats.

"Open the door, Pete," Louis said. Then: "No more meetings till I get in touch with you. *Nobody knows anything.*"

10 Marks felt they were onto something the minute he and Tomasino walked in on the Little Brothers. He could feel the tension, see the tautness in the faces that didn't know whether to grin or grimace. They had walked in on a council of war, a trial of a member, something like it, something with discipline. He glanced around the cellar. The only light, a naked bulb, hung from the ceiling over the green poker table. A few folding chairs stood against the wall. They were courtesy of Rossi's Funeral Parlor. On the wall itself the American flag was draped alongside the green, white, and red flag of Italy. Marks approached the youngsters, walking behind Tomasino, taking in what he could while Tomasino explained their visit: checking out all the clubs to see if anybody had seen anything unusual on the streets the night before.

Marks tried to evaulate the difference in attitude here from that in the other two clubs they had visited so far: it was in the degree of alertness, concern. It could be fear.

The fat boy was trying to set a smile and it wouldn't hold. The youngster next to him kept his eyes down. None of them looked curious, the primary characteristic of the other clubs. A handsome youngster with delicate, almost feminine features was the color of putty. The big fellow next to him got up and shook hands with Tomasino, the *macher*, Marks thought, and all of them straightened their backs from his example.

Tomasino introduced him: "Lieutenant Marks, this is Louis Fortuno."

Marks avoided the hand offered him by scratching his neck

at that point. Let Tomasino take care of the amenities. "How old are you, Louis?"

"Eighteen."

"Occupation?"

"I got a scholarship to play football. I'm a student."

"Congratulations," Marks said. "Any of you know Ben Grossman, the shopkeeper knifed last night on Hester Street?"

"It depends on what you mean by know, lieutenant," Louis said. "We know there was a shop there run by an old man, and we heard what happened." He nudged the boy sitting tense as a cricket beside him. "Get a couple of chairs, Angie."

The boy moved like a sleepwalker. Marks watched him. When he brought the chairs, he was shaking so badly he couldn't open them. The chief was about to take over. Marks motioned him to stay where he was.

"What do you do, Angie?" Marks asked, taking a chair from the boy, opening it for himself and putting his foot on it. Tomasino did the same thing.

"Nothing, sir," Angie said.

"Nothing?"

"Sometimes I work in a bakery." Then, in a cry that was downright pathetic, "I'm going to be a dancer."

Louis picked that up like a dropkick. "Hey, brothers, did you hear the kid? A dancer, Angie, and you never told us."

The gang laughed too loudly. The boy returned to his place, a chair without a back.

Marks pointed at the fat boy. "What do you do?"

"I work on Fourteenth Street, Butchers' Row."

"A butcher's apprentice?"

"Not till the fucking union says so." Bravura.

"What's your name?"

"Ricardo Bonelli."

"Bonelli?" Tomasino repeated tentatively. "Didn't I see the name on last night's blotter?" He had gone over the precinct record.

"Yeah, I guess. The cops carted my old man off to Bellevue

last night. He was drunk and we got in a fight. He tried to throw me out a window."

A piano would have been easier, Marks thought. "What time did all this happen?"

"I guess I could figure it out," Bonelli said, "but I wasn't looking at my watch if that's what you mean."

"Figure it out. We're in no hurry."

"Look, lieutenant," Louis put in, "this is a private club and we're having a peaceful meeting. What I mean is, do you have a warrant?"

"And what I mean is, wouldn't you rather talk here than in the stationhouse?" Marks spoke amiably, something he did not feel like doing. These punks were more self-righteous than a temperance outfit.

"Okay," Louis said. "I just want it on the record."

Marks took out his notebook. "It goes in the record." So far, he had nothing to go on in any suspicion of these youngsters except their own reactions, but in his estimate they fit Grossman's "baby fascists." "Now, young Mr. Bonelli, what time?"

"I was thinking the police would know the time better than me. I mean the neighbors called the police and they called the ambulance. There'd be a record on that, wouldn't there?"

"Give me an approximate hour."

"Twelve-thirty. I got to be in bed early. I clock in on my job at four A.M. The old man was drinking. We don't get along so good then. He fell asleep in the couch watching T.V. and I lay down on my bed with my clothes on. When he woke up like at midnight, he wanted me to go out and get more wine and when I said I wouldn't he took a swing at me. He's been real mean since he got hurt on the job."

"When was that?"

"Five years ago maybe. I was a kid."

"Did you go for the wine?"

"Yeah, and by the time I got back, he didn't want it. I got so mad I hit him over the head with the fucking bottle and that's when the old bitch next door called the police."

Louis said, absolutely straight, "We got a regulation in the Little Brothers, Bonelli, and you know it. That language don't go in this room."

Marks would have laughed if the scene had not been so grotesque.

He went round the table, leaving Angie to the last, and took names, addresses, and statements. All the other Brothers were able to account for their whereabouts from ten o'clock till dawn with remarkable recall. They had all, in effect, kissed their mothers goodnight and gone to bed long before midnight. Except for the dancer. Angelo Palermo lived at home, but he had not stayed at home last night. He had watched the making of a movie on Grand Street. About eleven o'clock he had gone to what he called his hideout on a tenement roof.

"Were you anywhere near Grossman's shop?"

"It must be two or three blocks."

"Who are you hiding out from, son?"

Angie shrugged. "I just call it a hideout. I look at the stars and things."

"What's wrong at home?"

"My mother's got a man. I mean, I'm in the way."

"No other family?"

"My brother's in the marines. My father's in California."

"Did you stay on the roof all night?"

"No, sir. I got kind of scared, imagining things. What I did—I went to a restaurant where there's a girl I know. On Houston Street. I stayed with her."

"All night?"

The boy nodded. He wasn't meeting Marks' eyes, only skittering glances as though to see if the detective was buying his story.

"What's her name?"

"Alice."

"Alice what?"

"I don't know."

"And the name of the restaurant?"

"I don't know," he said, almost a whisper.

Bonelli came to his rescue. "I can tell you he was there, lieutenant—till half-past three anyway. I saw them on my way to work. I got to walk, you see. Sometimes a prowl car gives me a lift, but not last night, so I seen him and the waitress. It's a dump called Minnie's Place."

To Angie, Marks said: "'Did you see Bonelli?'"

"Yes, sir."

Were these two alibiing one another? Had it all been worked out in anticipation of police questioning? Marks was not going to find out talking to them together. He took the whole group by surprise. "Okay, Brothers. That's it for now." Without another word he walked out. Tomasino followed.

Behind the wheel of the car, Marks asked: "What makes them different from the other gangs we've seen tonight?"

"Something, but they're not bad kids. A little self-important maybe."

Marks started the motor. "What do you think was going on when we walked in?"

"A ritual of some kind. The Little Brothers call themselves a secret organization. Maybe they were initiating the kid on the stool."

"By scaring him to death?"

"I'll make a guess at what was going on, Dave. They're a pretty puritanical outfit. I'd say Bonelli had informed on the kid, him being with this chick, Alice or Minnie or whatever. That's alien territory over there. Maybe they were putting the screws on the youngster."

Marks didn't buy it, but he did not say so: he merely made a mental note that when it came to Tomasino's old neighborhood, the young detective went on the defensive.

As they stopped at the intersection of Mulberry Street and Broome, a police car wheeled around in front of them, its occupants caught briefly in Marks' headlights. It was Sergeant Regan and, if Marks was not mistaken, his passenger was Julie Borghese's roommate, Phillips. He glanced at Tomasino, about to mention it, and then decided to go it alone. Tomasino was lighting a cigarette, unaware of the car that had turned in front of them.

Marks pulled in to the curb. "Tommy, take the car over to the stationhouse and leave the keys at the desk. I want to walk off my suspicions—or re-inforce them."

Marks did not drag his feet as he headed toward Julie Borghese's, but neither did he run. He did not want to draw attention. He even spoke a word along the way to one and another of the women who sat outside, fanning themselves. Some still wore black, but most of them wore bright colors and the dominant language was English. First generation American.

The squad car was parked a few doors away from Julie's. The two men were still in it. If it was Phillips, what did it mean? That he had remembered something concerned with the homicide and checked in locally? That he had decided he could make identification? Marks had felt from the first that there was something fishy about Phillips. It made him hesitate now, and while he hesitated, Phillips got out of the car and went into the building. Marks had a good look at him in the vestibule light.

Marks reached the squad car on the driver's side just as Regan started the motor. "I thought it was you," Marks said, putting his hand on the door.

Regan peered out at him. "What's new, lieutenant?"

"I was going to ask you the same thing."

"Not much. It's a quiet neighborhood—most of the time. Anything on Grossman?"

Obviously Regan had no intention of mentioning Phillips. "Not only quiet—it's closed. Nothing new," Marks said.

"Can I give you a lift?"

"No thanks. Goodnight, sergeant."

Marks strode away. He now had anger to walk off. Or else he could find some pretext to confront Julie and Phillips again. His pride would not allow that, no more than it had permitted him to ask a direct question of Regan. Their business probably did *not* concern him. He had his anger to walk off, nevertheless.

11 Louis had warned Angie not to go home until he got over the shakes. He was not to worry about the cops, just stick to his story. He'd done fine. But Louis had wanted him out of the clubhouse in a hurry: that was the only thing Angie was sure of. It made him feel like a leper, an outlaw. He didn't know which he longed for more, his bed or his hideout. He knew, but Louis' order made him choose the hideout.

He had the ladder up within a rung of the roof when a violent wrench pulled it out of his hands. He looked down to see the detective steady it on the floor and start up. Angie was trapped. Alone and so soon. Lieutenant Marks stepped onto the roof and shone his flashlight into Angie's face. Then he snapped off the light.

"Let's pull it up and put the door back. Isn't that how you work it?"

"Yes, sir."

"Then do it," Marks said, when the boy made no move.

When the door was in place the cop turned on the flashlight again. He threw its beam over the rooftop, letting it linger on the tent. And then on the bucket. Angie's heart beat even harder.

Marks said: "So that we won't get into any misunderstanding, go over and put your hands against the wall above your head." He motioned with the light. Angie obeyed, placing his hands against the brick of the warehouse that backed the tenement building. The cop's hand crawled around his waist, under his arms and down his legs. Angie kept thinking of the sand bucket with the knife in it.

"Are you always this scared of the police, Angie?"

"No."

"Then what's it all about? Your heart's going like a trip-hammer."

"It shook me up, you coming up the ladder like that."

"I see. May I take a look?" Marks had already squatted down at the opening to the tent.

"Sure."

The detective explored Angie's supplies, not missing a thing, edible or readable. He pushed aside *Portnoy's Complaint* to see the book beneath it: *Outdoor Survival*. "Have you ever been in the country?"

"Once. To my uncle's chicken farm in New Jersey."

"Where in New Jersey?"

"I forget. We took a bus over the George Washington Bridge."

"Know anybody in Weehawken?"

"No, sir."

Marks straightened up. He threw the beam on the sand bucket.

"If I got to pee," Angie managed.

Marks turned off his light and walked to the parapet.

Angie moistened his lips as soon as he got enough spit in his mouth. He went after Marks, but slowly, and he put his hand to his heart where it was beating so hard it hurt.

Marks looked at the building across the way, saying nothing for a long time. There were lights on in a lot of the windows, including the girl's where the one shade was drawn as far as it would go and the other down all the way. In the next apartment two men in their undershirts were playing backgammon. Down one floor, a woman was diapering a baby on the living room rug. "So this is where you were—from what time on last night?"

"Eleven, a little after."

"Did anything special happen over there, something I could check out your story against?"

"I can't think of anything."

"Try. These are easy questions, Angie. We can go to the hard ones if you want to."

Angie knew he had to tell him something, and he couldn't just make it up. He decided to tell the truth—up to a point. "There's a girl who lives where that blind's three-quarters down—with the plants on the fire escape?"

"Yes." Angie could see his profile, that was all.

"I saw her in the movie they're making on Grand Street. I mean I knew where she lived and everything, so I was watching for her to come home."

"And?"

"They came in—her and a man—and pulled the shades like they are now."

"Doesn't she always pull the shades?" the cop asked, quick as a light.

"No, sir."

"What happened then? Something—to keep you here till three in the morning."

Angie wanted to empty himself of the whole story, the theft of the coat and plane ticket. The cop was going to pull it out of him, bit by bit.

Marks said, "Was that the first time you'd seen the man over there?"

"Yes, sir." It occurred to Angie then that the cop already knew . . . And Angie had put the coat in the locker: that would prove something in his favor.

"Between twelve and three, Angie?"

"I was pretending something. It's hard to explain."

"Try. I've done some pretending in my day. I know what it's like to be sixteen and think about a girl. I know what it's like to be thirty-six and think about a girl. How do you like that?"

Angie was wary, but what could he say? "I pretended the man was somebody important in the movies. I pretended they

94

came up to the roof over there and I was dancing. I don't know how but they could see me . . . I know it sounds crazy, but I really did dance."

"And they came over and got you and took you to Hollywood and you became a star."

"Crazy," Angie said again.

"Not the dream part, but here's what's crazy, boy: your saying in front of the Brothers tonight that you were going to be a dancer."

"It just came out."

"Nothing just comes out. You're scared, my boy, that's why it came out. What's it got to do with Grossman's death?"

"Nothing!" But his voice cracked on the word.

"Okay. How did you get into that club in the first place, the Little Brothers?"

"They're all right," Angie said.

"You're somebody's patsy. Do you know what a patsy is?"

"Not exactly."

"It's a fall guy, somebody who does the dirty work, who gets the blame."

Angie didn't say anything. He was afraid in his guts that it was true, Ric getting him in the club and everything, and then the way Louis wanted him out of the place quick. But he did not know for sure. What he did know was that the cop was trying to soften him up.

"Am I wrong?" Marks asked finally.

"I don't know."

"But you do know how you got into the club in the first place."

"Somebody recommended me—Ric Bonelli." Angie felt better just saying the name.

"Peculiar, wasn't it, him happening to come along in time to see you in the restaurant?"

"Yeah."

"What time was that?"

"Three-thirty."

"How is it you're so sure of the time?"

"My mother goes to work at five. If I was going home before she got up . . ."

"I see, but you didn't go home. You stayed with Alice."

"That's right."

"Then I guess I'd better talk to Alice, wouldn't you say?"

"Yeah . . . sure." Angie tried to sound more willing.

The detective left him at the parapet, but he turned on his flashlight and went back to the tent. Angie ran after him. It was like a terrible game, the detective getting closer and closer to the bucket. This time he touched the bucket with his foot. Or so Angie thought. He was not even sure, but he panicked.

"Lieutenant, there's something I got to tell you."

"That's better," Marks said.

"It's easier if I show you from the edge," Angie said, and Marks returned with him to where he could point out the girl's fire escape and the steps that led up to the roof. He managed to pour out the whole story except that he took the blame for selling the plane ticket himself. He even told how he'd run away and left Alice in the bus depot.

"Where's the coat now?" the cop asked when Angie paused, thinking he might not have to go any further. He had said he was returning it to the man.

"It's in a locker he'd rented in the bus station. The key was in the pocket."

"And what was in the locker?"

"A black suitcase . . ." The priest was going to have to take care of himself. "It wasn't locked so I opened it to put the coat inside. He's a priest."

"What?"

"I saw the breviary and the Roman collar."

Marks laughed aloud and Angie hated him almost as much as he hated himself at that moment. "I'm not laughing at him—or at you. I was just thinking of the little things that trip a man up, the best and the worst of us. So everything's back in the locker—except the plane ticket?"

"Yes, sir. Even what was left of the money."

"And the key?"

"I got to find a way to get it to him. I don't even know the girl's name."

"Julie Borghese." The cop stood, one foot on the parapet, an elbow on his knee, and stared over there. Finally he rubbed his chin between his forefinger and his thumb. Angie could hear the rasp of his beard stubble. "Let's have the key, Angie. I'll give it to him and you can work the rest out yourself."

Angie had never known such relief as came with this token restitution and the sight of Marks striding across the roof. He kicked aside the hatch-door and dropped himself down to the floor below, ignoring the ladder. Angie watched until he went into the building opposite. Then he got the knife from the bucket, fastened it to his belt inside his jeans, and started for home.

12 Marks was well aware that he was using the boy and the key as a pretext to crash Julie Borghese's. Granted the validity of checking the boy's story, he should have brought the youngster with him. No, in that, he decided, he was being harsh on himself. Admit that he was infatuated with Julie Borghese and let it go at that. He understood now Regan's circumspection. Phillips would have gone to the stationhouse and confessed his predicament to a Catholic officer. Understandable, if you understood a vow of celibacy.

He knocked on Julie's door and got no answer. He knocked again and said aloud, but not too loudly, "It's Lieutenant Marks, Miss Borghese."

Julie opened the door on the latch chain.

"I have something for Mr. Phillips, a key to a public locker."

"He's not here," Julie said.

Marks did not believe her, but decency forbade his saying so. "Then you can give it to him."

"I don't want it, but thanks just the same."

She was about to close the door. He now believed her to be alone, hurt, he suspected, and angry. "Please . . . I'd like to verify the boy's story. It may connect with the homicide."

"Where's your partner? Don't you come in pairs?"

"Not this trip."

She slipped the chain from the latch and let him enter. Marks closed the door and then said, "Or shall I leave it open?"

"Don't overdo it, lieutenant. I know all police are perfect gentlemen."

"That's an old-fashioned word."

"Isn't it?" she said, even more sarcastically.

There was no one else in the apartment. Phillips had taken off either while Marks had paced the street to Houston and back or while he had followed the youngster up to his rooftop. The girl's morale was low and she made no attempt to conceal it.

Marks nodded at the Virgin ascending. "That's the one you bought from Grossman. Right?"

"Right."

"I wonder what he thought."

"I know what he said: Esprit de corps."

"Ach," Marks said: he glimpsed another facet of the dead man and this one hurt, somehow. "So there was humor underneath—a musician with humor."

"I didn't know he was a musician. I mean it never came out to me."

"A long time ago."

"His humor didn't come out often either. Sit down if you want to. Between the fan and the window—that's the coolest place."

"I'll try not to intrude any more than I have to," Marks said and forgave himself the hypocrisy. "But I want to tell you about a sixteen-year-old boy who's been watching you from the roof across the way."

Julie sat near the fan and lit a cigarette. Marks sniffed the smoke when the fan blew it his way. Julie said, "It's not pot, Lieutenant Marks."

The detective lit a cigarette of his own and repeated Angie's story. He omitted the fact that Angie had discovered the man to be a priest. It occurred to him that Julie might not know that.

"It's straight," she said, "as far as it goes. I picked him up on location, as they say in movie jargon. A movie buff."

"A film editor, I thought," Marks said.

Julie's very blue eyes met his. She knew. She fought back the tears. "What do you want, Lieutenant Marks?"

He smiled wryly. "At the moment, to say I'm sorry you got hurt. Which is none of my business."

"That's right, man."

Marks described Angie.

Julie said: "There are a lot of handsome youngsters in Little Italy."

"But this one has a crush on you. Of course, all the others may too."

"Not all," Julie said with the faintest of smiles.

"What I'd better arrange," Marks said, "is a viewing at the precinct house in the morning. Angie runs with a group that calls itself the Little Brothers. And there's a boy among them that Phillips might have been describing this morning. Do you know where I can reach him?"

"Father Phillips? Oh, yes. The rectory of St. Patrick's down the block. He'll have checked in by this time."

"Then I suppose I can give him the locker key myself."

"He doesn't need it, lieutenant. With his magic, he can open every locker in the terminal."

"I should have thought of that," Marks said. "He's in for a shock when he opens the suitcase and finds the coat inside."

"Ha!" Julie's eyes screwed up and she smiled at the picture he had conjured for her.

"But no plane ticket. However, the boy did leave him some of the money."

"I'd like him to get back every penny of it," Julie said.

"I understand."

"No you don't. How could you? A casual pick-up—a priest? Who cares nowadays?"

"The priest himself."

"Yeah, you got it exactly. The way he went out of here, mea culpa-ing—it made me feel like a whore. And I'm not. I'm not even casual. I liked him."

"I didn't," Marks said. "I'm not sure why I disliked him so

much. When I saw him get out of the squad car earlier tonight and come up here, I could have killed him. Mind you, I didn't know a thing about him then. I just felt that he wasn't up to your caliber. But if I hadn't felt that way, and hadn't marched up and down the street trying to figure out what to do about it, I wouldn't have spotted the youngster and I wouldn't have got the story."

"So gallantry pays off."

"Is that what it was?" Marks got up and put his cigarette out in the ashtray near Julie.

"He is a film editor. Besides the other business. He teaches film."

"Okay. It doesn't matter much, does it?"

"I guess not. I ought to feel sorry for him. Instead, I'm feeling sorry for myself."

"Pride," Marks said.

"Is that what it is?" She gave him back his own words mockingly, and Marks remembered her doing the same thing with Regan in Grossman's shop. "Would you like a drink?"

"I'd like to, but I'd better not, thank you."

"Oh, shit," Julie said. "Men *are* hypocrites. If you want a drink, man, have one."

"No, thanks," Marks said, feeling put down. "Ten o'clock in the morning at the bottom of Elizabeth Street. Shall I have someone pick you up?"

"Never again," Julie said, so that he left with laughter between them.

But on the way downstairs he was aware of his first twinge of sympathy for Phillips.

13 Marks headed for the precinct house by way of Hester Street. The entire Grossman building was in darkness, including the third-floor apartment where the windows were opened wide which added to the look of desolation. It surprised him, how little activity there was on Hester Street. It was going more and more to factories. And scheduled for urban renewal. Some of the buildings were already vacant. Marks by-passed the clean square of glass which still bugged him, and looked into the shop through the padlocked door. The broken statuary lay in a box near the door. It occurred to him that if it had been the killer who turned the shop into its present state of chaos, the technicians would have an easier time of it. There was something discouraging about tackling a clean house: so Mattie, the woman who had worked for his mother since Marks' childhood, always said. It was at this point he remembered that it was Friday night and that he had promised to attend a dinner party at his parents'. He looked at his watch. It was almost ten. Neither the first nor the last of such delinquencies.

He crossed the street to the entry of the leathergoods factory. The light was too dim for him to read the notice on the door, but he assumed it announced the vacation closing. There was a crackling sound among the debris beneath his feet, not paper . . . He stooped down and groped gingerly. Conscious of the third-floor windows across the way, he did not want to use his flashlight. Peanut shells. He had recently seen whole peanuts . . . it came to him where: among Angie's supplies in the tent, a plastic bag of them. While he remained squatting, thinking about it, something caught his eye, a whiteness, a movement at one of the Ruggio windows? There was nothing more and it might have been the flutter of one of the pennants strung across the street. He remained achingly immobile and studied the window. Instinct, nothing else, suggested that somebody up there was watching him. He did not move. A car passed, the beam of its headlights just missing him. Allioto was closing up the delicatessen. Earlier than last night. Was he frightened? On the side streets there were people, but not a soul on Hester. His legs grew numb. A sound he didn't identify immediately: then, a baby starting to cry, its first cries muffled as though it had wakened on its stomach. The crying picked up in strength. Marks saw the movement at the window. The watcher gave up the vigil to go to the child. A light came on. Marks stood up and massaged his legs, but without taking his eyes from the window. The child stopped crying. He saw neither shadow nor person and very shortly the light went out again.

Ruggio might have come home, but Marks doubted it. The feeling of a lone woman watching in the darkness was very strong. He went to the phone booth on the next corner. Information got him the number of Alberto Ruggio and the operator dialed it for him. He let the phone ring eight times and thought of the woman nursing the child. No one answered.

He contacted communications. Nothing yet on Ruggio.

He decided it was worth the manpower to keep the Grossman premises under surveillance for the next few hours, and having arranged it, waited himself for the arrival of the first detail. As the minutes dragged on, he thought of the loneliness of a one man job, the stakeout. His was one of the last of the solitary police operations. Even the patrolmen, for the most part, walked in pairs. He had himself once thought that all Manhattan was his beat. In his college days he had walked the city day and night, never thinking he would become a policeman. Like his father and his grandfather, he had studied law, but he had not practiced. He would not have made a good lawyer: even now he was hung up between prosecution and defense. Which ought not to make for a good cop either, although he was well aware he was so regarded by the men at the top.

At the precinct headquarters Marks asked the desk officer if he might see the record of the previous night's complaints. He studied the entry on Bonelli. A Mrs. A. Niccoli of 1893 Elizabeth Street had called the police at twelve:forty-five. The patrol car reached the scene seven minutes later. Bonelli, Senior, was lying in the third-floor hall, unconscious and bleeding from a head wound. An officer had called Bellevue Hospital, and while waiting the arrival of the ambulance, had taken a statement from Bonelli's son, Ricardo Junior. He had pushed his father, who was trying to get him back into their own apartment, and his father had crashed through the railing to the floor below. Junior had stayed with him until the police arrived. The complete entry: this was not the way Ric had told it at the clubhouse. In the context of the Grossman case, there were many unasked questions: how long a time elapsed between the beginning of the quarrel and the end of it? When was the window broken? How long was Ric out of the house, presumably getting wine? Where did he get it? Where was he at eleven-thirty, which was the approximate time Phillips had seen a boy whose description seemed to fit Bonelli? Nor was there mention of his hitting his father over the head with the bottle.

Marks asked the desk man if he had been on duty at the time.

"Yes, sir."

"Why wasn't an assault charge placed against young Bonelli?"

The officer turned the docket around and read it, trying to refresh his memory. "They must've figured it was an accident."

Marks said nothing. He remembered the boast very clearly, and the top Brother's reprimand for the obscenity.

"Any follow-up on the father's condition?"

There was none. Nor was there a statement from Mrs. Niccoli in the record. Was it all bad police work? Marks didn't think so. He had the feeling that there was a reason behind every apparent goof. He had a feeling: it was an expression the inspector hated. Then scratch it, he'd say.

Marks said, "There are six youngsters I'd like to screen for witnesses in the morning, sergeant. Can we arrange it here?"

"Give me their names and addresses and I'll set it up for you, lieutenant."

14 Only a few doors separated Angie's building from the one where Ric lived. When Ric was not at work, Angie always went around the block to avoid his building. Now he wanted to avoid Ric more than ever. He wanted to get home and hide the knife in a place where he knew it would be safe. But old Mrs. Niccoli saw him.

"Angie, come here!"

There was no sign of Ric. He went to her. She was a terrible woman, always picking at him for information about his mother, about whether his father got re-married, which meant divorce. Either way, he was living in sin. Angie knew she made fun of Mr. Rotelli to the other women, the way she imitated how he used his hands. She was sitting on her own chair on the sidewalk outside the vestibule. A couple of other women were with her, sitting on their own chairs. "Your mother isn't home," she said.

"Okay," Angie said. "Thanks." He didn't know what for, but he said it automatically.

"She went in a taxi with Mr. Rotelli."

"I know," he said, just to get away, and started for his own building.

"Ric's looking for you."

He couldn't bring himself to answer. He knew why he hated her the most: whenever he got past without meeting Ric, she was there to let him know he hadn't escaped for long. Halfway up his own stairs he met Ric coming down.

"Where you been?" Ric demanded.

"At my hideout." He wasn't ever going to tell Ric where that was.

"The Little Brothers are down on you, you know that, don't you?"

"I can't help it," Angie said.

"The cops coming in like that—and you thinking it was me on the phone. I bet you still think it was, right?"

Angie stepped on a bug and didn't say anything.

"I don't trust that guy Marks, the lieutenant. He's got it in for us. You can tell."

"Who's us?"

"Italians, I mean. The other guy, you could tell even from him. My old man's still in the hospital. Let's go over to my place."

"I'm too tired."

"We got to talk private."

There was no one home at Angie's either, but he did not know how he would get Ric out of the house once he got in. He couldn't count on his mother coming home early on a Friday night. He went back down the stairs ahead of Ric and put his hand to the knife to make sure it was securely sheathed inside his jeans.

Mrs. Niccoli said, "How's papa, Ric?"

"Coming along fine, thank you." Ric said it like a Little Brother, Angie realized. Halfway up the stairs, Ric muttered, "The old bitch." He stopped at the next landing. "Right here's the spot where they folded him up on the stretcher." Somebody had put in a larger light bulb than Angie had ever seen in a hallway before. There were dark stains on the floor, probably wine, but they looked like blood. Ric stepped under the light. He stuck out his arm and pulled up the sleeve. "Look."

Angie saw a deep, angry scratch. He thought instantly of Mr. Grossman's cat.

Ric was watching his face and he liked what he saw. He laughed as though he was going out of his mind. "Where do you think I got it?"

Angie shrugged. He couldn't have got the words out if he'd had to. It was another of Ric's old tricks, only the situation was a lot different. I dare you, Ric was always saying for as long as Angie could remember him: I dare you to tell on me, always knowing Angie wouldn't, even if he had to take the blame himself. But the scratch was real.

"From the bottle when it broke," Ric said when he stopped laughing. On the next landing he pointed out a repair in the railing. "That's where he tumbled over. I don't care. He had it coming to him. He never lets up on me. From a little kid—'You mother-killer.' How'd you like somebody saying that to you all the time?"

"I wouldn't," Angie said. He didn't think he was going to be able to stand it if Ric started that story over again that night, about his mother's death when he was born. Angie wanted to think about the scratch, but not while he was with Ric. He wanted to get off by himself and think out what really happened at the Little Brothers' if he could. From the point where Louis started asking Ric questions. Everything changed when the cops came. He waited while Ric unlocked the door. Maybe Ric had wanted the cops to come, to pin Angie down. Maybe he'd called them too. Ric, the informer. Angie wished he could take out his knife and put it to Ric's back and say, Tell the truth. Ridiculous.

The lights were on in the Bonelli apartment. It was filthy, especially compared to Angie's. There were dirty clothes on the floor, and paper plates with stale food on them and flies all over. The glass still lay by the broken window.

"My sister used to try and make it up to me sometimes. Then she'd get mad at having to take care of me. Now she's such a rich bitch she won't even come home on San Gennaro's Day. Jesus, how I hate them all."

Angie chose a plain, unupholstered chair and sat down carefully. The upholstered things were full of stains. He discovered that he had to sit up very straight because of the knife.

"I hate them," Ric repeated.

"Me too," Angie said, meaning that he hated his mother, but not his father.

"If it wasn't for the Little Brothers . . ." Ric left the sentence unfinished.

Angie thought he understood something then: Ric needed the brotherhood. Something that had come to his mind several times during the week came up again: he wondered why the Little Brothers, who were so exclusive, wanted Ric if nobody else did. "Who did you have to put the Killing Eye on, Ric?"

"Why?"

"I was just wondering."

"The shoemaker, Rocco. He beat his kids. And you want to know what happened to him? You know the shop, how it goes down the steps?"

Angie nodded.

"He tripped and put his head through the glass door. He lost one eye. An eye for an Eye. It was a big joke."

Angie couldn't laugh, and he felt Ric must have done something to make it happen. Something real. He remembered Louis asking him on oath if he had killed Grossman. But he still didn't know what he'd wanted to find out about Ric; he should have asked who recommended him. Some day he'd ask Tony maybe.

"Who do you think killed Grossman, Angie?"

"I don't know. I don't want to know."

Ric squatted at the edge of a sagging chair. "Take a guess."

It was as though Ric was trying to get him to accuse him. "Maybe the big guy who lives upstairs maybe."

Ric looked about to spring at him. "What do you say that for?"

"I'm just guessing," Angie said. "I told you I don't know. The colored man maybe."

"What'd he look like, the one you saw?"

Something had changed in Ric in just that few seconds. "What'd he look like?" Ric said again.

This was the very point, Angie realized, at which the police had interrupted. He wanted terribly to understand. God . . . a breath's length of prayer. He shrugged again and felt a shift in the knife. He folded his arms. He knew he was sitting like a statue, and in that instant he remembered something that made Ric's story at the clubroom a lie: the black man wouldn't have been carrying the statue out in the open. He'd have had it wrapped up or in a box, the way Angie had seen him carry whatever it was he took from the shop. Even if it had dropped and broken, the stuff inside would not have spilled on the street the way Ric had told the Brothers.

"Black people all look alike," Ric said, and he was coaxing, "but something, you know . . ."

Angie said, straight out of his Forty-second Street experience: "He was wearing a little gold earring."

"That's the guy!" Ric said. "Big, yeah?"

Angie nodded.

"The same one. I knew it. I might've told the police that day if I hadn't got wise all of a sudden to why they didn't stop, and am I glad now I didn't."

"Why?" Angie felt his first little flex of power.

"Like Louis said, if it's the Mafia and you get in their way, you're dead. It's all right the way it is. It's great. I mean, Grossman's taken care of. That's the big thing."

"I guess so," Angie said.

"I don't dig you. He was in drugs, right? You're the guy that proved it. I don't mind, I mean, it was your Ordeal, and it happened."

Angie drew a deep breath. "I don't think the Killing Eye had anything to do with him being killed."

"You better believe it, Angie."

"Unless somebody was watching me watching him and caught on."

"Okay. Isn't that the Killing Eye? What'd you expect, a miracle or something?"

"But if it was the Mafia, wouldn't they be after me?"

"You can't be sure," Ric said. "Could you identify the cops you saw getting paid off?"

"I only saw one," Angie said. "No."

"And lots of niggers wear earrings," Ric went on, contradicting his own certainty because it suited him. "But once you put the Eye on Grossman—and the nigger caught you looking in—he wasn't going to come to Grossman anymore. That put the Jew out of business. But he knew too much. So the mob sent him into retirement. That's how the Little Brothers see it."

Angie wasn't ready to believe it, not on Ric's word now. He knew that Ric had lied, but he didn't know why, and he didn't know what to do with the information. "How come they're down on me then?"

"That's something different," Ric said, "but I think I got you out of the noose. I explained it was like you had to have some kind of alibi just in case. That waitress you called Alice? The Little Brothers don't stand for her business. If she was in our territory, she might even be eligible for the Eye."

"Why?" Angie knew, but he said it anyway. All of a sudden, he was angry.

"Look, I'm telling you, kid, and I don't want none of your flack. She's a whore, that's why."

"You're a Goddamned liar!" In that instant he was not afraid of Ric. He clenched his fists, wild with rage at the dirtiness, the meanness, Ric getting back at her because she called him Fat Boy.

"Hey," Ric said, a silly grin spreading over his face, "you mean it. You're really sore at me. She must've give you a free ride, huh?" Ric slid his tongue around his lips. "I won't tell. You balled her, huh?"

Angie was mute with rage. The words raced through his mind, but stuck in his throat. He reached beneath his belt and unclipped the sheath.

Ric slipped off the chair and bounced like a huge ball. He kept jumping up and down like a fat clown with the grin painted on his face. The very windows jingled.

Angie pulled the knife out. He hardly knew he was doing it. Ric went into the motions of a boxer, dancing around him, feinting punches, ducking, wheezing, dribbling spit. Angie made little stabs in his direction, but his feet were like stones, holding him in the one place. For the first minute, no longer, he could have killed Ric, but with that minute past, he was only defending himself. The terrible dance went on, Ric going into a wrestler's act now, crouching, heaving his shoulders, popping out his belly, bumping things out of his way with his rump, kicking over chairs, grunting, howling. Angie put the knife away, stuck in his belt because he couldn't get it into its sheath. He doubled his fists and held them tight against himself for protection. Ric gradually calmed down to where he stood and panted for breath, the smirk coming and going as he sucked the air in noisily.

Angie backed to the door. He had to look to unbolt it.

"Angie, wait up."

He looked round. Ric hadn't moved.

"I ain't going to tell," Ric said.

"Tell! Tell the whole damn world."

"I mean about the knife."

Angie went out and closed the door behind him. He heard Ric's phone ring. He hoped it was some terrible news and then hated himself for the weakness that kept him from ever getting beyond the wish, the hope.

The first thing he did when he got home was hide the knife in one of his father's shoes which were in his closet. He could remember his mother pitching the pair of them out of the closet in her bedroom all the way into the living room. His father had forgotten them, or else he never meant to use them again, the ties that went up above his ankles. He hated them. "Like in the old country," he kept saying. But he had said it in Italian.

It was one of the things his mother and Angie never talked about, him keeping that pair of his father's shoes. And when she cleaned his closet, she never touched them. Angie could see the dust on and under them where she'd wiped around them. Sometimes he cleaned it away himself with a pair of socks he was going to put in the laundry. He pushed the knife down deep in the shoe so that it would not show, and flapped the tongue over the hilt.

He went into the bathroom. He could smell himself, the way he had been sweating all day. He drew a slow bath of tepid water and sank into it. He didn't know how he felt except tired and depressed. He had just left the bathroom when the phone rang. He was sure it was Ric, and if it was, Ric knew that he was home. He'd keep on calling.

"Angelo Palermo?" It was not Ric's voice.

"Yes."

"This is Sergeant Darcy at the Precinct house. Lieutenant Marks wants to see you here at ten:fifteen tomorrow morning."

15 The smell of the East River was pungent as Marks started up the FDR Drive, a low-tide smell that he liked, something just short of rotten. There had to be a reason for the blotter discrepancies . . . Did the clannishness of the neighborhood extend into the precinct police? He thought of Tomasino, his hesitancy to criticize the boys. Was that hesitancy compounded in the case of this Mrs. Niccoli? Might she have been afraid to substantiate her complaint against one of the Little Brothers? He thought again of Angie and his fear in that bleak clubroom. And on the roof: Marks could not believe the theft of the coat sufficient to generate that kind of fear.

He tried to remember himself at sixteen. He understood the prevalence of fantasy very well. What was his *Portnoy*? Mailer. He remembered hiding *The Deer Park* in his laundry bag, of all places . . . and Mattie shaking her black finger in his face when she found it. The laundry bag: whoever killed Grossman would have gone from that hallway a bloody mess . . . Why did the butchery of the cat seem so much more terrible than that of the man? And it did in a way. Its gratuitousness? Would a cat defend its master? Young Bonelli was a butcher's apprentice—or would be when the union made room for him. A hoister of beef: he would wear a coat or a smock at his work, and at the day's end, it would be as bloody as the carcasses he hauled.

Marks was approaching a vast complex of buildings on his left. He realized that he was about to pass Bellevue Hospital.

Bone weary, he nevertheless took the next exit from the Drive.

Dr. Noble looked more harassed than noble, Marks thought, as what resident in a city hospital did not? While he talked, he now and then brushed his hair from his damp forehead with the back of his wrist as though to keep his hands clean. Marks asked him if Bonelli had been drunk on arrival.

"With the concussion, it's hard to tell. But the blood tests and urinalysis don't show excessive alcohol."

"Just how severe was the blow on the head?"

"When a man of his weight lands on his head after a fall of twelve-fifteen feet . . . he was lucky. He could have broken his neck."

"Doctor, let me get this straight: I've been told he was hit on the head with a bottle."

"I don't know where you got your information, lieutenant. Unless we're talking about two different men. I treated Bonelli for a nasty bump which, I was told by the ambulance nurse, came from his falling down a flight of steps. And that's what the wound looked like. I can assure you, if I'd seen anything else in the X-rays, I'd have reported it. People sue these days at the drop of a hat—or a head. The concussion came from the fall."

"I'll be damned," Marks said. Now he understood why there had been no arrest record at the precinct. But why had young Bonelli fabricated such a story? "Can I talk to the patient?"

"Absolutely necessary?"

"If it wasn't, I wouldn't be here," Marks said. "I've worked round the clock myself."

"I was thinking of the other patients in the ward," Noble said, "not Bonelli. He'll go home tomorrow. There's some of them won't ever go home."

"I'll keep my voice down."

Noble hung up the Bonelli chart.

Marks asked: "Does that show the nature of a work disability he suffered a few years ago?"

"The X-rays show it: the spinal . . ."

Marks interrupted: "Give it to me simple, doctor. Tonight I won't get it otherwise."

"He can't lift any weight to speak of."

"Lead me to him. He's supposed to have tried to throw a two-hundred-pound boy out the window last night."

"Some boy," Noble said. They went down the passageway past several wards where only the night lights shone. The doctor checked the names on an open door, using the nail of his little finger as a guide. "Bed number six—by the window on the left."

"Thanks." Marks nodded to a man with his bedlamp on. He was reading from a prayerbook, his lips continuing to move while he looked at the detective. Marks thought of the numerous paintings of St. Jerome, for the praying man's cheeks were cavernous, his complexion gray.

Bonelli lay on his side, his back to the door. Marks went around the bed. His head was not bandaged, but bruise marks showed on the forehead and cheekbone and beneath his eyes. His eyes were closed, his breathing even. A big man with a mustache as dark and heavy as a shoebrush. There was nothing ascetic in that face, Marks thought. He laid his hand on Bonelli's shoulder. The man came instantly and violently awake. He tried to roll off the bed.

Marks pinned him down. "Take it easy, Bonelli. I only want to talk to you."

"Who are you?"

Marks identified himself.

"I don't know anything," Bonelli said. "Let go my arm."

"You won't try to get up?"

"I was having a bad dream."

Marks let go of his arm. "Your son doesn't look much like you."

"Ric? His brother looks like me. Ric and his sister, they look like their mother."

"Is she dead?"

"With Ric. He was too big."

"Was it a bad quarrel last night, Mr. Bonelli?"

"I don't talk about last night. I forget. I hit my head and I forget everything."

"All right. Let's start earlier." Marks settled his backside on the radiator. There was no chair. "What kind of an accident was it in which you hurt your back?"

"I was a construction worker."

"Who did you work for?"

"Different people."

"When you got hurt?"

"Rosetti Brothers."

"Ever hear of the Ambrose Corporation?"

"Sure."

"Any connection with Rosetti?"

"Mr. detective, I am a worker. Why don't you ask a boss?"

"That's a good idea," Marks said. "Has Ric been around to see you?"

"Tomorrow he comes."

"What I'd like you to tell me—quietly so that we don't disturb the other patients—is just what happened between him and you last night."

"You ask so many questions. Answer me one question: how come you ask all these questions? The cops from Elizabeth Street, they don't make trouble. You I never seen before. What do you want from me?"

"I'm a homicide detective, and I'm investigating the murder of Ben Grossman on Hester Street."

A single swallow. Which told nothing really. Then: "When was the murder of this Ben Grossman?"

"Last night or early this morning. Did you know him?"

"I heard of him."

"What did you hear?"

"He sells religious articles. A Jew, you know? So people talk."

"Now tell me about you and your son last night."

He was in no hurry to start, and when he did, Marks suspected he had gone on the defensive about Ric. "He's a good boy to his father. Sometimes we fight, but it don't mean so much. His sister took care of him, both of us till she got married. My back. Now I keep house like a woman. Ric and I don't get along, sure. It's no good, two men alone."

"Last night's fight," Marks said evenly. "What was it about?"

"Ask Ric. He don't get the bump. Don't ask Ric. He makes up things."

"Who broke the window?"

"I gave him a shove. It broke."

"Why?"

"I think I wanted some wine. That's what it was about. So he went out and got the wine, and when he comes back, I don't want it no more. So we fight again. The neighbor knocks on the wall—Niccoli, she is one goddam gossip. Ric rushes out the door and I try to stop him. I don't want trouble. All of a sudden, I'm falling downstairs and after that I don't know till I'm in the ambulance."

"Ever have any business yourself with Grossman?"

"I got no business with that man. No business."

"Do you know a lawyer by the name of Gerosa?"

"I hear the name."

"Where?"

The man tried to shrug. "Maybe somebody suggests him when I get hurt on the job."

"Do you know anyone in Weehawken?"

"My son, John—he lives there. He's a lawyer. Maybe that's where I hear of Gerosa, from Johnny."

"How long was Ric gone from the house when he went out for the wine?"

"I don't know. Five minutes. Ten."

"Long enough for you to forget that you wanted it," Marks said dryly.

"That's right." And Bonelli Senior showed his straight white teeth under the black mustache. He had picked up confidence.

Marks got up. He was too tired himself to know whether he was being taken for a fool or talking to one. The man with the prayerbook had closed it, his finger in the place where he had been reading.

He said, with a ringing clarity, "Bonelli, you're full of shit. All night long you keep every man in the ward awake swearing you have a pig for a son, a no-good pig who wouldn't come to see his father, only if he was in the coffin."

"You shut up down there. My Ric is all right. Last night I hurt my head. I don't know what I say."

"But you know now what you feel in here." The man tapped his chest.

"I know, but you don't, so shut your mouth and say your prayers."

Every man in the ward came awake, a babel of eight tongues. Marks beat his retreat hastily.

He decided before he left the hospital that he would not go home, that he would catch a few hours sleep on a cot at squad headquarters. The big boss, Inspector Fitzgerald, did not like this mode of work, his obsessiveness in some cases. Except that the old man called it possessiveness and meant the word. "You act as though you own some homicides, Dave, and you don't. They belong to all of us." It had been said with his particular sarcasm. But this case *was* different, and Marks did feel that he owned it.

The Bonelli story was going to have to be checked out minute by minute. It was the obviousness of young Ric that disturbed the detective, what looked like a weird kind of showing off, even to the kind of braggadocio with which he told of his job. He wanted attention: was that it?

Marks was about to pull up to a shop for coffee when he remembered Alice's restaurant—Minnie's Place, according to Ric. Houston Street was not far.

When Marks walked in the shop was empty except for the waitress. She was putting on nail polish. "Hi. I'll be with you in a minute—unless you're in a hurry." She checked her hair, which was closer to orange than to blond or red, with the inside of her arm. It put him in mind of Dr. Noble.

"No hurry," Marks said. "Is it always this slow?"

"Friday night," she said. "You'd think it was a religious neighborhood. I figured on closing up as soon as my nails dried. Eggs or a frankfurter? The hamburger I'd skip if I was you."

"Just coffee," Marks said.

She blew on her nails to dry them and then put the bottle of polish in the cupboard under the cash register. She took his full measure in the back mirror. "A cop?" she asked when she turned around.

Marks nodded.

"On or off duty?"

"Half and half." He made a pass at his I.D. carrier. She didn't want to see it. "What's your name, miss?"

"Gertrude Abramovitch."

Which all but destroyed one of Marks' surmises, that she was a part-time prostitute. Who in that business would keep the name of Gertrude Abramovitch? "Somebody said it was Alice."

"Somebody?" Her guard went up.

"Angie. I guess you could say Angie sent me."

"That's mean of him. After what I did for him."

"Don't jump to conclusions, miss."

"Did he tell you about last night?"

"More or less."

"Half and half, more or less. He did or he didn't, officer."

"He did, but I want to hear your version, and I do need a cup of coffee."

She poured him coffee that was hot, if not fresh. "He came in wearing this sports coat that didn't fit him too good, and we got talking. I'd rather talk than almost anything."

"What time did Angie come in?"

"About three, let's say. Then about three-thirty, along comes this fat guy who turns out to be an acquaintance of Angie's."

"I want everything you can give me on him."

"A pleasure, only I wish I knew something. He's a big sour pickle, a natural-born bully. Angie didn't tell me this, but I'd bet you the doorkey this Fat Ric beat up on Angie his whole life. You know the way a dog gets hand-shy? That was Angie when this fatso got anywheres near him. Which is why I let Angie take me home. I mean we made out like we already had a date, Angie and me, because I knew he was scared to death of this big klutz."

"Did he tell you why?"

"No, he couldn't, I don't think. It's kind of psychological, I figure. Why is anybody scared of a bully? If they knew, they wouldn't be scared anymore. Right?"

"Right," Marks said.

"I figured at first there was some connection about the coat. What'd he tell you about that?" She darted the question at him, and blew on her nails, waiting for his answer.

Marks laughed at her attempt to take him by surprise. "He told me he had stolen it, and that he cashed in the airlines ticket so that he could take you to the Palisades Amusement Park today."

"No kidding. He told you that? Did you arrest him or anything?"

Suddenly Marks had it the way it had actually gone: Alice had been the one with the savvy to convert the ticket into cash. She could carry it off; he doubted that Angie could. "No. In fact, I've helped him to return the coat to its owner."

"The funny thing is, officer, the Palisades Amusement Park isn't there anymore. We couldn't have gone to it anyway. Somebody told me that in the bus station, and I was going to say to Angie, we could go to Radio City Music Hall, or Coney Island, which was where he wanted to go in the first place."

"Why didn't you?"

"So he didn't tell you he run out on me?"

"Not in so many words. I think he was afraid he might involve you in whatever trouble he's in."

"You make him sound like a real Don Quixote. If that's who I mean."

"I thought him a Sancho Panza type," Marks said.

Miss Abramovitch looked at him blankly. It was not who she

had meant. "Anyway," she said. "I came out of the booth in the ladies room and some dame was screaming like she was being raped, you know? All Angie'd done was open the door wide enough to throw the shopping bag in where I'd find it. He'd put some money in it for me. Did he tell you that?"

Marks shook his head.

"He's a funny little guy. I'm kind of falling for him again just talking, but a girl don't like to be stood up by somebody younger than her."

"Why do you think he did it?"

"What I figured out—he'd been saying maybe he ought to call his mother. That's what I think he did while I was in the john. There's something not exactly kosher there. I mean Oedipus or something like that."

Marks grinned. He had been sitting, chin in hand, his eyes half closed while she talked. Thus he was able to see her breasts through his lashes without seeming to stare at them. "What time of day was it?" he asked almost dreamily.

Miss Abramovitch thought about it. "Eleven this morning, say."

By then the newspapers were on the street, Marks thought. He pulled himself out of his reverie. "Tell me every single thing you can remember about the fat boy."

"Ric something—belly. Bonelli."

"Yes."

"Well, for one thing, this big black sweater he was wearing, like it was winter, and the way he waddled down the street when I was setting the night lock on the door. He looked like a Santa Claus, you know what I mean?"

Marks caught the image at once. "Too fat in the middle?"

"That's what it was like. Like he was stuffed with a pillow or something. He could hardly get his hands in his pockets."

If Ric Bonelli was the killer, Marks thought, he could indeed have worn a butcher's smock. That had already occurred to him. And he could have used a professional's knife. "Do you have a phone, miss?"

"I got one at home and I might as well close up and save on the light bill."

Marks looked at her wryly, his brows arched. "All right. I'll give you a ride home."

"That'll be nice, and call me Alice. I kind of like it. Angie made it up."

16 Marks arrived at Division Headquarters shortly after seven. He had had five hours of solid sleep and a good breakfast. Since normally it would have been his Saturday off duty, he made short shrift of matters that did not pertain to the Grossman case.

The file had built overnight.

He swore aloud as he read the top report: the men assigned to track down Ricardo Bonelli's work clothes had taken a short-cut: they had gone directly to young Bonelli to find out where he worked. In that way, they were able to complete their exercise in futility before knocking off their tour of duty on time. From the office manager of the provision company, they learned that the regular laundry pick-up was at noon on Friday. By five in the afternoon the batch of smocks which would have included Bonelli's had gone into a detergent vat in the Bronx Industrial Laundry.

Since neither Marks nor anyone else on the case had heard of Bonelli in time to have done anything about that, there was no blame to be placed for it. What irritated Marks was that Bonelli now knew the extent of Homicide's interest in him while potential evidence had gone down the drain, so to speak.

The interim report from the Medical Examiner showed that the tiny shreds of wool beneath the cat's claws came from the chest area of Grossman's sweater. A marked photograph accompanied the report. Marks tried to imagine that final scene in the man's life. Had he been trying to protect the cat, holding it in his arms? The knife wounds had been in

124

Grossman's back; he had fallen forward, but he had rolled over or been rolled over. The only certain thing was that the cat had participated in some way that brought on its own slaughter.

Marks was glad to turn to the reports of the first and second details on the stakeout: no action except the brief appearance of a woman near the window at a quarter to six that morning.

From Center Street: the FBI had no record on Ruggio. Which was not what Marks had asked: he had merely wanted them to facilitate his queries with other government agencies.

Marks dialed the Ruggio number again. Ten rings without an answer. He rang almost as long trying to get a telephone operator. He asked for a tracer on any outgoing calls. That the operation was automated meant it would take time. But it also meant a record.

Tomasino had written up the Gerosa statement before going off duty. Marks read it through and then sat thinking about Grossman's shift from one notorious concentration camp to the other . . . where he had been able to commandeer the musical talent of a communist internee. And others? Two men did not make an orchestra.

He decided to talk to his father about it. Julian Marks, a noted trial lawyer, was active in politics and philanthropy, and well-connected in the state of Israel. He was an early riser while the detective's mother was a heavy sleeper, but when Marks phoned, he got the maid who was neither, but who loved her "Davie."

She was sufficiently awake to tell him about the dinner party he had missed the night before. "You promised your mother, Davie."

He always promised his mother, rarely attended, but generally called to offer his last-minute regrets. He now went through the part of the ceremony which applied when he had not called. Nor did it matter whether he spoke to Matty or to his mother: they worked it out together. "What did I miss, Matty?"

"A very nice young woman, a Ph.D., but not too brainy."

His mother had a way of bringing out the eligibles. "Too bad," he said.

"I'll get your father. It's very early, Davie. Have you been to bed?"

"Yes, Matty, I've been to bed."

He told his father about Grossman, detailing mostly the Gerosa information. Then he found himself reviewing the case as he saw it to the hour. "There's a little square of clean glass in the shop window that keeps nagging at me. A window within a window. Somebody said yesterday it was like a frame where he was supposed to see a face that would haunt him."

"That sounds very Christian to me, Dave."

Marks laughed.

"I should think if it was a matter of justice—or of vengeance—it would have happened long before this. And more directly. An eye for an eye, a tooth for a tooth—nothing devious about that. But I'll find out if there's anything on him one place or another. What time is it now in Haifa?"

"Two or three in the afternoon."

"Some hours before sundown."

"Oh, Christ," the detective said. "Do they keep the sabbath that strictly?"

"Allah is even stricter," his father said.

Detective Westcott's report on the Ambrose Corporation showed it to be an importer of food products, which Marks knew from his ill-managed visit to the warehouse when he had let Ruggio disappear on him. The firm had been incorporated in 1959, taking over the assets of a bankrupt company that had been around since 1912, Amalfi Brothers. The Ambrose record was pristine. Westcott suggested that since the original deal had been made in cash and property, if there was Family in it, it was well concealed. The time was right: the date coincided with guarded Family entrances into legitimate businesses. There could be an ex-mobster wrapped up in its respectability.

Westcott's reports always read like carefully researched theme papers. Marks blessed him for it. He had dug into the history of the building on Hester Street. It had come to the Ambrose outfit in the Amalfi package, purchased in 1933 by Rudolph Amalfi for $46,000. Which, Marks realized, was the exact amount Grossman had paid for it twenty-seven years later. That could not be coincidence. Irony, maybe. Something quirky. The property had been appraised at $72,000 in 1933: Amalfi had got himself a Depression bargain. Why had Grossman got himself an even better bargain in a seller's market? Then he remembered Gerosa's words: Would you say today he got a bargain, lieutenant?

Westcott had done both a genealogy and a business précis on the names connected with the firm. Thus, he showed that Bruno Rosetti, a director of the Ambrose Corporation, was also a partner in the Rosetti Construction Company, the same company for whom, it was safe to assume from the name, Bonelli Senior had been working at the time of his back injury.

An evaluation of Grossman's legitimate business showed that while on the surface the absence of receipts and vouchers might suggest carelessness or conversely carefulness, the more likely explanation seemed to be that he turned over all his receipts and records to someone else, a part of the operation involving the eighty thousand dollars in the safe. Duplicates of his import vouchers were on file with the customs office, in the files of the shipping carrier and in those of a cartage firm. The market for religious articles was more lively on paper by far than on the Hester Street premises. The retail value of Grossman's total imports came to just under $30,000 in ten years. To have sold as many statuettes as he had purchased, he could have placed at least two in every home in Little Italy—where nobody bought by Grossman.

Marks wrote a memo to Westcott to get together with Wally Herring, who was covering the narcotics angle for the division.

Tomasino checked in, his tie hanging out of his pocket. He was disappointed to see Marks in ahead of him. "I didn't even stop for breakfast, for Chris' sake."

Tomasino sipped coffee from a plastic cup and Marks

brought him up to date as they drove to Elizabeth Street. They stopped on the way to confer with the stakeout. The stakeout car was a beauty: two crumpled fenders and a dented door with cracked window-glass. There had still been no traffic to or from the upstairs apartment. And Mrs. Ruggio was not answering the phone.

"Or else they have an arrangement," Tomasino suggested. "Only answer if I hang up for a beat and dial again. Something like that."

"Possible," Marks agreed.

"Why not put an all points out on him?"

"Not yet."

"What do I do if she does come out, boss?" the stakeout asked. "Do I follow her?"

"If she has the baby with her, yes. Otherwise not. But I don't think she'll come out, maybe not till she rots."

"Jesus, you're cheerful this morning."

Marks was watching a milk truck deliverer set out four cases in Allioto's doorway. Baby Ruggio was on his mother's milk. She wasn't going to run out of that right away. "Hang in," he said to the man on watch.

"With five kids, what's my option?"

Marks grinned. "Six."

There was country music playing behind the Bonelli door as Marks and Tomasino passed on their way to see Mrs. Niccoli. Tomasino called attention to the unpainted repair to the railing. He smelled the wood. "It's new," he said.

Mrs. Niccoli was an old woman with sharp black eyes and, Marks soon learned, a tongue to match. She began on Tomasino before they got in the door. "Why don't you live in the neighborhood anymore, Tommy?"

"What's so great about living here? My folks still live here. Can we come in for a minute?"

"At my age a minute is worth something, but come in. Your father don't make such good suits no more. For the politicians maybe. Not for the people."

128

"All the people want is a First Communion suit—out of a pair of pants."

She cackled with laughter and Tomasino pinched her cheek. He introduced Marks.

The country music penetrated the walls. "What went on in there last night, Mama Nicco?"

"Noise." Then, disparagingly, "Them." She went to a table covered with a lace cloth where an electric coffee pot was percolating, the room filled with the aroma. She pulled out the cord. Imperiously, she gestured them to sit down and brought a coffee cake from the sideboard. "I like a good fight—a man and a woman. Then you learn something, how much money he makes, how much she spends and for what, if he's been faithful. If he brings it up, last night he was faithful. If she brings it up, you don't blame him. When two women fight, it's better than television. But them. Like two bulls. It makes me sick. You're not Italian." The last sentence to Marks without a change of inflection.

Tomasino answered, "He's got an Italian heart, Mama Nicco."

"That don't cut no shit with me, Tommy. What do you want?"

"We're investigating the homicide of Grossman, the shopkeeper on Hester Street."

"Mama Niccoli knows nothing. Help yourself to the cake." She poured the coffee.

Tomasino served himself and Marks. "Then let's talk about your neighbors."

"*Them?* No."

"Why not, Mrs. Niccoli?" Marks said quietly.

She looked at him coldly. "How is he?"

"I saw him in the hospital last night. He'll come home today."

She gave a sigh he could not interpret.

"They haven't always been bad neighbors, have they?" Tomasino took over gently.

"Once . . ." she started and cut herself off. "That's the

truth, Tommy. Ric . . . even him." Then she let go: "I'm an old woman. I got nothing to lose. When I'm blind, it won't matter I don't have a window. Sometimes I feel sorry for Ricardo the father. When you can't work, you don't make bargains, believe me. He put a son through college, then law school. What a party there was last winter when Johnny got his license. And a year ago when Marguerita got her rich husband. But where are they now, the rich Bonellis? Sub*ur*bia." She made a beautiful Italian word of it. "It's not like the old country, no sir. And Ric? Everybody's punching bag, all his life. Nobody likes him. His father don't like him either. And that's what he wants—why doesn't he like me, Mama Nicco? From a little boy. What do you tell him? Find somebody else you can make like you. Papa loves me, papa loves me, papa loves me. He used to say that over and over, playing by himself in the hall. What else can I tell you, Tommy?"

"What time did they start fighting last night?"

"I couldn't hear the eleven o'clock news for them. I knocked on the wall. It was quiet and I went to bed. They woke me up—I don't know what time . . ."

"You called the police at twelve:forty-five," Marks said.

"So."

"Over a bottle of wine," Marks prompted.

"A bottle of wine," she repeated.

"From Mike's place?" Tomasino said.

She shrugged. "Where else at that hour?"

"And I suppose they'd have fought over money," Marks said as though he himself were reminiscing.

"Always . . . No, not always, but nowadays every single time."

Marks said, "And the Jew?"

There was the faintest beginning of confirmation. Then she straightened up, out of the reverie. "You go to hell, Mr. Detective, whoever you are."

Marks got up. "Sorry, Mrs. Niccoli. Thank you for the coffee."

"Bah!" And when Tomasino followed Marks to the door, a piece of the coffee cake still in his hand, "Shame on you, Tommy."

"We got a dirty job to do, mama."

"You don't do it to me no more."

In the hallway Tomasino jerked his thumb toward the door to the Bonelli apartment. Marks shook his head. He wanted to try for Phillips' identification first.

They walked to Mike's Bar, less than a half block away. Mike had a barrel from which he drew wine for the locals. It was closed at that hour of the morning. No matter for now.

Tomasino went on to the precinct house. He was to see that Allioto showed up for the lineup, an inexact term in this instance, but it was what the occasion would amount to. Marks drove to St. Patrick's rectory. He had seen no point in confiding Phillips' identity to Tomasino. The priest was in the clothes of his office when he came into the small parlor where Marks waited, studying the photographs of the last three popes. The difference in Phillips was striking: a self-assurance, but without the taint of arrogance which Marks now took to have been self-protection. They shook hands and talked for a few minutes. Neither of them referred directly to where they had met before, but it was important to Marks to explain that certain of the boys he wanted Phillips to view might well be implicated in Grossman's murder. And that was all he said of the boys.

"Let's go," Phillips said.

"There's no hurry. Julie will be there. So will the delicatessen owner."

Phillips smiled. "Are you saying there's time for me to change into mufti?"

"I guess that's what I had in mind, father."

Phillips shook his head.

Julie and Allioto arrived within a couple of minutes of one another, and Marks placed them along with Phillips behind a

131

one-way mirror in a glass-partitioned office with a view of the entrance, the desk, and the lobby. The normal routine of the stationhouse went on uninterrupted.

The Little Brothers were punctual. No group of youngsters, according to the desk officer, was more cooperative with the police than the Little Brothers. The last to arrive was Ric. He was sullen and silent except for something he said out of the side of his mouth to Angie. The smaller boy moved away from him. Ric followed him. Marks let them wait for five minutes to allow his witnesses a full viewing. Louis joked with the desk officer. The others spoke among themselves and now and then said a word to the men coming off or going on duty.

Allioto felt that he had seen them all at one time or another, and he knew Ric and Louis from their having brought in the flags he displayed in his store window. He was pretty sure that the round-headed boy with the short haircut had collected a donation from him for somebody who couldn't meet their rent and was facing public assistance.

"What if you hadn't been willing to donate?" Marks asked.

"I don't think I'd 've got a knife in my back," Allioto said.

Marks persisted. "What would have happened?"

Allioto thought about it. "Maybe a few cartons of milk would go to the poor in my name."

"Robinhoods," Marks said without enthusiasm. He turned to Phillips. "Father?"

"The fattish boy could have been the one I saw, but I will not swear to it."

And that was that.

"Who's the slight, sweet-looking boy?" Julie asked. "I've seen him before."

"Where?"

"I don't really know. Just . . . around."

"Near Grossman's?" He was leading the witness and Marks knew it.

Julie said carefully after a moment's thought: "I don't ever come farther downtown than Hester Street." Then: "That isn't true either. I often go to Chinatown for dinner."

"He's your voyeur," Marks said.

"Is he? I don't think I mind."

"I'll arrange an introduction," Marks said dryly.

"He owes me pretty close to a hundred dollars," Phillips said, "and God knows I could use it."

"St. Patrick's is a poor parish, isn't it?" Julie crooned in mock sympathy.

"What does that mean?" He was hurt, but he'd asked for it.

"They must have more priests than they need to go round."

Marks said, "Especially when the Little Brothers get there first."

Allioto, whom they had forgotten for the moment, laughed. So did the priest.

Marks asked them to wait until the Little Brothers had gone and thanked them for coming in.

He went out the back door of the room and around through the corridor. He told the boys that they could go and even managed regrets for having got them up early on a Saturday morning. Louis glanced at the room with the mirror. It was an incongruous piece in so antiquated a setting. Louis knew, but he did not say anything in Marks' presence, and the boys started to leave. At the last minute Marks called Angie back.

17 As Angie turned back, Louis said: "Hold it, Brother. See the mirror in the room over there? It's a phony. He's got a witness back of it who maybe identified you, so watch yourself."

Angie did watch himself as he followed Marks to the stairway. He tried to think, but his mind kept getting stuck on the words, Watch yourself. How could you watch yourself except in a mirror? He knew what Louis had meant, of course, but he didn't know what to do about it, so he let the words keep repeating in his mind.

Marks took him into an empty room where there was a long table with chairs on both sides, empty of people. He sat where Marks told him to. "Louis is one smart fellow, isn't he?" the detective said.

"I guess he is."

"Miss Borghese identified you, but she couldn't remember from where."

"I could identify her too," Angie said.

The cop snorted, not exactly a laugh. Then his eyes turned dead serious. "You like peanuts a lot, don't you, Angie?"

"Yeah, I guess I do." Whatever he had expected, it wasn't that. He waited for the number-two punch.

It didn't come. Instead, for no reason Angie could guess unless he suddenly had to go to the bathroom, the detective got up and left him. All he said was that he'd be back. Alone in the big room with its green walls and the iron-meshed windows through which a muddy sunlight oozed, Angie felt he was already in prison. There was a bulletin board with notices and photographs of wanted people. He could get up and look at it. Nobody said he had to sit there in one place. He did get up, but only for a second: there was something about sitting still that made him feel safer, more inside—something, he did not know what. The room was terribly big.

Peanuts. He did like peanuts. He had a plastic bag of them in his hideout. He'd seen somewhere that they were a very nourishing food. He'd decided that if he had to choose one food for survival, he'd take peanuts. Not salted, but in the shells, natural food. Sitting hunched up, waiting, hearing the distant sound of voices, the more distant sounds from the street, motors taken quickly up in speed, all seeming to go away, and feeling himself caged in when he almost wished he *was* caged in, he thought what it would be like to be a monkey. He began to scratch his head, for it did itch, and then his back and under his arms, his ribs. It was crazy and yet it made him feel better; he not only got up, but he climbed on the chair and then onto the table. He jumped up and down and hammered his chest, moving very quickly from the smaller of the species to the larger.

"Get the hell down from there, kid. What do you think you're doing?"

A uniformed cop had come in, a Chinese boy with him. The Chinese kid hung back.

"Come on, down to the other end," the cop said to his prisoner.

Angie wondered what the Chinese kid had done. Marks returned just as he sprang off the table, his weight on one hand.

The detective stared at him, his hands on his hips, a humorous, questioning look on his face.

"Jumping up and down like a goddam monkey," the cop at the end of the table said. "King Kong." He turned to his own prisoner and said sarcastically, "If you'll excuse the expression."

Marks didn't answer him; nor did his prisoner except with a hate-filled dart of the slanting eyes.

Marks motioned Angie to sit down and then sat beside him. "Peanuts, right? From peanuts to monkeys?"

"Yes, sir."

"We ought to find something more constructive to do with that imagination of yours—before you do something *destruc*tive. Unless you've already done that." He waited.

So did Angie.

"Angie, how would you like to level with me if I level with you? I know you're in some trouble that connects with Grossman's murder. The Little Brothers are tied into it and you're up front in a way I *don't* understand. You seem like a nice kid. Are you covering for Bonelli? What?"

Angie shook his head. He did not dare look at the cop, the way he was coming closer and closer.

"Tell me this. I know you've been around Grossman's lately—did you notice a patch of clean glass in his window?"

He started to shake his head again and realized that the girl might have seen him there. "Yeah, I did." He tried to sound as though he had just remembered it. "I even looked in the shop. I don't know why."

"What did you see?"

"An old man teasing a cat with his finger."

"Now that we're in the neighborhood, Angie, what were you doing at the entrance to the factory across the street?"

The peanuts. He remembered eating them there during a vigil, and there had been so much junk on the ground, he'd emptied the shells out of his pocket. "I was going to try and get a job there, but it's closed for the summer." He had once intended to do that.

Down the table the cop was making a lot of noise, slamming down a chair, shouting, trying to scare the Chinese kid who sat, silent as a stone. Angie wished he was like that: he talked too much and fidgeted.

"How long do you think Ric Bonelli would cover for you, sitting where you are now, Angie?"

136

Angie shrugged. Ric would have to, on his Little Brother's oath.

"Don't you see he's using you for a cover to what he did Thursday night? He didn't beat up on his father, he didn't hit him over the head with a bottle . . ."

"I know," Angie said. "I mean I know Ric brags a lot."

"Something that strikes me as damn peculiar, boy—at the very time you were supposed to be dancing on that roof, your friend Ric was somewhere in the area, somewhere between your hideout and his house. He wasn't home, Angie. You know that too, don't you?"

Angie's heart began to pound again. "No."

"Dancing on a roof—who the hell do you think you're kidding?"

"It's the truth."

"Didn't you steal that coat for an alibi?"

"No."

"Why did you tell me about it then?"

"I was scared."

"Of what?"

"You. I'm just scared of cops. That's all."

"A Little Brother? They love cops, Angie. They think they are cops."

"But I'd stole the coat!"

The cry came at a moment of silence down the table.

The Chinese boy raised his voice, the first time Angie had heard it: "Get a lawyer!"

Before Angie realized the words were meant for him, the cop down there shoved his hand over the boy's mouth. Just for a second. The cop pulled his hand away and began to scream, "You yellow-faced son of a bitch, you don't bite an officer and get away with it." He began to shake the kid as though he could make him fall apart.

Marks said to Angie: "Go on. Get out of here."

Angie went without looking back. The kid couldn't have heard him if he had said thanks. Ordinarily, Angie did not like the Chinese although he was not afraid of them the way some people in Little Italy were; they just weren't his idea of American. And they smelled so different. But he wished that he could help the boy and hoped that maybe Marks would.

As soon as he got out of the stationhouse he went looking for Louis Fortuno. He found him at the Police Athletic Gym near the old cathedral. Louis was in gym clothes, skipping rope, counting every skip. His eyes recognized Angie, but they didn't welcome him. There were several men watching Louis. They didn't pay any attention to Angie. One of them had an unlighted cigarette dangling from his lip. It was like an old movie on television. The place was air-conditioned, but it smelled of Louis' sweat.

Angie waited for Louis to go through a whole workout. Then Louis, in bathrobe, introduced Angie to somebody he called "Coach" as the fastest kid in Little Italy. "You ought to clock him."

"Mañana," the coach said. He couldn't have been less interested.

Angie followed Louis into the shower room.

"What are you doing here, Palermo? I got a college career to protect, and maybe a lot of money if I get picked up by the pros."

"I got to talk to somebody."

"Not here."

In the end, they talked as they walked back and forth like two novices in a passageway between the gym and another building. Angie had rehearsed himself on how he was going to start about Ric, but he started on himself. "I was supposed to stay with Grossman, you know, the Ordeal—till midnight. Right?"

"So?"

"I got scared and left at eleven. And now the lieutenant says Ric could've been there after that."

"And what did you say?"

"Nothing."

"So what do you want from me, a knighthood or something?"

"It's just that Ric lied to you about the black man dropping the statue and all that. He couldn't . . ."

Faster than he saw it coming he felt the back of Louis' hand across his face. "I don't want to know!" Louis shouted.

"I don't either! I never in my whole life wanted to know anything about Ric, but he made me."

"Look, I could wipe up the floor with you, Angie. I'm sorry I hit you but you got to understand: the Little Brothers don't talk. I mean we cooperate with the police, but in a case like this you can't even trust them. You saw the cop with Grossman. And when it comes to protection, man, you're not going to get it. I'm not going to get it, Ric won't get it."

"How come I had to put the Eye on Grossman then?"

"Somebody opened a can of worms. I ain't saying who because it's too late . . ."

"Only I'm supposed to pick 'em up."

Louis gave a snort of laughter and put his arm over Angie's shoulders. "I'm glad you're in the organization. I like you, Angie, and I'm sorry you got that particular Eye job."

"So am I."

"I'm going to tell you something I got from my confidential police source: they're after that guy, Ruggio, who lives upstairs with his wife and kid. What I think, when you put the Eye on Grossman and saw the black guy and the black guy figured you dug what was going on, Ruggio got orders to close up the shop, including Grossman—for good. The police got the place staked out, but Ruggio hasn't showed up since he went to work yesterday. Maybe he's wiped out too. And that scares me even more."

Somehow, that part wasn't scaring Angie. He simply could not in his bones believe in a Mafia. "Louis, if that black man is pushing heroin, and us feeling against drugs the way we do, I could tell the cops something about what he looks like."

"A gold earring, Angie? That's like saying he's got gold fillings in his teeth practically. Look, give it a couple of weeks to cool. I'll call a meeting, and I'll include you in."

Angie left Louis with a soft good-bye. Ric had been to the

captain about the black man with earrings—which description had come entirely out of Angie's imagination. Ric was defending himself to the Little Brothers in spite of what Louis said about the guy upstairs. Defending himself . . . or trying to make himself a big shot? He wanted to be captain after Louis. Something occurred to Angie that shook him up in a different way: man for man, the Little Brothers were not the smartest kids in the world, even Louis who was set for college.

18 Detective Herring had come on duty when Marks and Tomasino returned to division headquarters. "Here's something you might be waiting for, gents," he said without prior greeting. He read the State Department communication: "No record of immigration of or alien resident under name of Alberto Ruggio."

"Which confirms the suggestion that he entered the country illegally, doesn't it?" Marks said.

"Dig that legal jive. Good morning, boss."

"The same to you," Marks said.

Tomasino said, "And therefore a possible Syndicate import."

"With wife and child?"

"Family people have families like everybody else," Tomasino said.

"And the Ambrose Corporation—does that put them in the Family way, too?"

"Maybe yes, maybe no," Tomasino said.

"Who gets the social security checkout?" Herring asked.

"Let's have it," Marks snapped. He was in no mood for dribbles and maybes.

"It's *kosher*, but Albert, not Alberto."

"I'll be damned," Marks said.

"That's not only *kosher*, that's *chutzpah*," Tomasino said.

Marks corrected his Yiddish pronunciation. "I don't suppose they gave us the date when he got the number?"

Herring said, "What you don't ask, they don't tell."

But Marks was more interested at the moment in the

telephone company's report on one out-of-town phone call made from Ruggio's. It was made to an unlisted number in New Jersey at 1:35 A.M., Friday. Which had to be within an hour of the Grossman killing. It lasted under a minute. "He could sleep through a howling murder a few feet from his door, and then get up to make a phone call an hour later."

"Who did he call?" Tomasino asked.

"Unlisted, but I'm going to find out." Marks waited on the phone while the supervisor got him the information that the service for the Jersey number was billed to a legal firm in Jersey City, Galli and Frascotti. She gave him the number of the firm and volunteered that it was listed.

"Thanks," Marks said, but he neither felt nor sounded grateful. He shoved the phone away. "They're covering for a client obviously."

"Or the client of a client," Tomasino said.

Herring said, "Why don't you just dial the number and see what happens, Dave? Somebody comes on, try and sell 'em a piece of real estate. That's what some bastard did to me at ten-thirty last night."

Marks shook his head. "No more tipoffs to make us look further ahead than we are. How far did you get, Wally?"

"Almost twenty-four hours I've been waiting a call-back from the Narcotics Bureau. I've tried them four times. It's a deliberate stall somewhere along the line."

"Maybe they're trying to unload what they've got on hand," Tomasino said.

Nobody laughed.

Marks said to Herring: "Don't you have a contact?"

"Not on the inside. I got one or two on the outside, if you want me to try them."

"On the street?"

"Yeah, I guess you'd call it on the street."

"Hold off," Marks said. "If there's a wide spread to the operation, Narcotics may have to take it slow."

"Then why the hell don't they say so?" Herring said. "Why don't *you* try them, lieutenant?"

"Because I wouldn't get any further than you, Wally. Don't go paranoid on me. In fact, that's the best advice I've got for everybody, including myself. I'm pushing. We're all pushing."

"A bunch of pushers. Speak for yourself, man."

Marks grunted.

"Why not the all-points on Ruggio now?" Tomasino persisted.

"I'll think about it. You're on regular today, aren't you, Wally?" Westcott was off-duty.

"Till 6 P.M. and they're waiting for me over on Avenue D, a family shoot-out. We need rain, that's what we need, a nice cooling rain." Herring checked his shoulder holster and pulled on his jacket.

When he had left, Marks suggested that Tomasino and himself knock off for a few hours. "Like normal cops and see what catches up with us."

Tomasino wanted to go to a wedding. He was not long in departing.

Marks called his father again.

"It's too soon, Dave."

"I know. Are you playing golf this afternoon?"

"I could be persuaded."

"Got an entré to any club in North Jersey, dad?"

"I think I can manage one."

"Sign us up and I'll be at the house for you within the hour."

19 When Angie opened the apartment door his mother was sitting opposite it like a cat at a mouse hole. She had a rolled up newspaper in her hand which she tested for strength on the arm of the chair. Not a word.

"How come you're home early, mama?"

"I want to know what's going on with you, Angelo."

"Nothing."

"I'll knock your ears off if you tell me *nothing*. You had to go to the police station. Why?"

"I wasn't the only one. Ric was there, Louis . . ."

"I know Ric was there. He tells me. You don't. But you they keep to talk to special. What about?"

"If I seen anything they could investigate about the murder."

"Grossman, the Jew?"

Angie nodded. It was a wonder Ric hadn't told her that, too. But he wouldn't—just enough to sic her onto Angie.

"And what did you see?"

"Nothing."

"Tell me the truth, Angelo. The cops don't investigate somebody for nothing."

"I can't tell you. I can't tell anybody. It's my oath to the Little Brothers."

"What's the Little Brothers got to do with you stealing? With you going to a whore?"

"That's a lie. That's what Ric says and it's a lie."

She got up and took his chin in her hand, a grip that hurt, but Angie determined to take it without flinching. Her eyes went into his like screwdrivers. "I want the knife, Angelo. Where did you get it?"

"I bought it." He could hardly say the words with her hold on his chin.

She let go. "I want it."

"No," Angie said.

She flew at him, beating him with her fist and with the paper. The more he stood still for it, the harder she beat him, making noises as though it was her getting hurt. Then she started to kick at his shins. "No? You don't say No," she was shouting.

Angie pushed her. He couldn't take the pain in his shins.

She fell back more than she had to and huddled like he'd been beating her. Her mouth hung open, a look of wild surprise on her face. She staggered to the chair and plopped into it, and dropped the paper. She'd gone limp all over.

"You're father I always expected to hit me. Not you, Angelo."

"I didn't . . ."

"Not my little Angelo."

"I'm not your little Angelo," Angie screamed. He hadn't hit her, but neither had he ever before even pushed her to defend himself.

"Is that what you learn at the Little Brothers, to hit your mother?"

"The Little Brothers got nothing to do with it."

"Such good boys, good to their parents, respectful . . ." she crooned sarcastically.

"They are good!" Angie shouted, wildly loyal. His voice broke into falsetto.

"What is the meaning of good, will you tell me?"

Angie said nothing. He had to fight crying. When he hit the false note he hated himself even more than her.

"I asked you a question, what is good?"

145

"I don't know."

"That's what I thought. Even in school, they don't teach you that anymore."

"I didn't push you so hard . . . I didn't mean to . . ."

"All right, you didn't mean to, but you're changed so much—always such a good boy, the nicest boy on the street. I don't know, Angelo. Is it my fault? Is it because of Mr. Rotelli?"

"It's my fault," Angie said. "It's me."

"It's Mr. Rotelli," she said gloomily.

"He's all right."

"He's not all right at all. He wants my son to be a dancer. How dares he?"

"It's not him that wants it, mama. It's me. He's only trying to help."

"Don't you tell me what he's trying to do. I'm in this world a lot longer than you are. Don't you understand, Angelo, everything I do is for you? I want you to have something for yourself, not like your father and me. You're all I got left, and I think Rotelli's got money. Be nice to him for Angelo's sake . . ."

Angie was shaking his head. "Don't, mama, not for me." He had to get out of there. He could hardly get his breath. "Marry him, mama. I don't care. I'd rather if you wanted to. I can take care of myself."

"Look at you—you can take care of yourself."

She was trying to make him sound helpless. He had not said what he wanted to, not the right way. He turned and fumbled at the door. She reached it just as he got it open and pushed it closed. She put her arms around him in a way that made him think of Alice. But her muscles then tightened like a man's and she lifted him from the floor and whirled him around before she let go.

"Not till you tell me, where is the knife, you don't go out of here."

"I threw it in the river." It was what he intended to do with it . . . as of that minute.

"Swear by the Holy Virgin."

"I swear, I swear, I swear!"

She went all soft again. "Look at me, darling, the tears I'm holding back. Look and you'll see them." She came to him, her hands outstretched.

He could not look at her face, he could only slyly measure his chances of getting out the door.

"Look at me," she said again. "When you were a little boy you used to sit in my lap and let me look at myself in your eyes."

He gave her his hands and then squeezed hers so hard his own hurt.

"Angelo, I don't sleep with Rotelli. It's not like that . . ."

"I don't care!" Angie shouted.

She shook his hands in fury. "You dirty, selfish boy! You want a whore for a mother—is that what you want? Maybe you bring her men, hah?"

"Sicilian bitch!" He hurled the words at her at last and pulled himself away.

She began to cry in earnest and Angie went out, not waiting to close the door behind him. Her sobs and wails followed him down the stairwell as he ran, faster and faster, until he reached the street and had to slow down because he could not see for the tears in his own eyes.

"Poor little one, poor little one," Mrs. Niccoli crooned as he passed.

From the top floor window Ric called down to him, "Angie, wait for me."

He ran again, stumbling, repeating to himself every dirty word he had ever heard in his life. He reached his hideout, half-expecting it to have been destroyed by the police or the hatch locked up, but nothing had been disturbed.

He was no wiser an hour later for having gone over and over in his mind, unable to stop, the things his mother had said. He was never going to understand her, and he didn't care, he didn't want to care. No wiser, but somewhat soothed by self-sympathy and solitude. The roof became very hot. He went to the parapet where there was a breeze. He sat there, his back to the street, to the girl's window. He didn't care about her either. He began to fantasy himself as an outlaw, as a man wanted as a criminal who hadn't even committed a crime. Then he heard his name called out in a girl's voice, a real voice, and looked across the way.

Julie was leaning out over the plants, her hands cupped round her mouth. "I'm coming over to see you, Angie. Fix it so that I can come up there."

20 The doorman was watching for Marks. He gave him the message that his father wanted him to come upstairs for a few minutes, and took over the car. Marks assumed something had come through on Grossman. His father opened the door to him and led the way to his study, a room off the vestibule before it opened into the vast living room. Marks caught a glimpse of Matty in the kitchen at the far end of the apartment.

"Mother's off. She wants you to have dinner here if you don't have a better offer," his father said.

"Not so far," Marks said. "You got an answer on Grossman, yes?"

"Yes, I got nothing," his father said, sitting down at his desk and turning on a second lamp. Marks could not think of a circumstance in which he would be hurried. "Now let me interpret that nothing for you. Your mother won't like that shirt."

"She bought it for me."

"Did she? I keep forgetting she can oblige both twentieth- and nineteenth-century tastes."

"Ben Grossman," the detective prompted.

"Mmmmm." His father put on his glasses and then took them off again. For many years he had resembled Toscanini. Now that he was showing his age, the features broadening, but his white hair still a dramatic shock, Ben Gurion came to mind. He was always being taken for someone famous, but not for the famous attorney he actually was. "What it means, Dave, no dossier has ever been compiled. In other words, he was not charged with collaboration."

"Probably because no one lived to accuse him."

"I wouldn't say that. He likely did a good deed here or there along the grizzly way. More to the point, he did not do a bad one. A weak one, yes. He would have cooperated to the extent of saving himself, but not at the expense of his fellow victims."

"In other words, he entertained Nazis but he did not fiddle Jews into the gas chambers."

"I would say so."

"You wonder then why he was changed from one camp to the other," Marks said. "I've assumed it was due to the wrath of his brethren."

"More likely it was a change within the camp command. He was undoubtedly someone's pet Jew."

"That sounds filthy."

"I like to say things like that, David. It's my way of making sure that we never forget. Now. Whoever is on the door will have put my clubs in the car. Shall we go?"

"I want to stop in Jersey City to check an address . . ."

"No, David. On the way home if you must, but not until we've had our game. This bit of investigation I've done for you would have taken a week through regular channels. I'm entitled to your undistracted competition . . . and my usual handicap of course. Tell Matty what you want for dinner."

"She knows." In the hall he called out a greeting to the woman in the kitchen. "I'll be here for dinner, Matty."

She came, wiping her hands on her apron, to see them out.

"Where did you say Mother was?" Marks asked as his father put on a jockey cap he always wore in the sun.

"Why, she'd be at a musicale at the Alice B. Toklas Hall." Which was the other side of his father; the Alice Tully Hall in Lincoln Center.

21 "It would have been a lot easier for you to come to my place," Julie said as she took the last step onto the roof.

Angie offered her a helping hand too late. He pulled the ladder up and closed the door. He could hardly believe the girl was standing on his turf, that she'd come to his hideout. Now that he could take a really good look at her, he could not bring himself to do it, only a glance now and then. "I'm sorry I stole the coat," he blurted out.

"I don't know whether I'm sorry or not. All sorts of things seem to be happening as a result. My name is Julie."

"Angie."

"I know," she said and held out her hand.

He gripped it firmly, as she did his. They both let go immediately as though it wouldn't be right to hold on any longer.

"I don't have chairs or anything. You'll get dirty."

She was wearing white ducks and a striped blouse that looked Italian. "There's always the laundromat," she said, and looked round for the best place to sit.

"I hate laundromats," Angie said.

"So do I. I keep hoping some day I'll meet somebody interesting in one, but so far they're all blobs." She sat in the shadow of the tent, her knees to her chin. Angie could see her sandaled feet. Neither her toenails nor her fingernails were painted, which he liked. He sometimes wondered what people would think if his mother's red polish chipped off in the bread dough and they found it.

"Were you at the police station this morning?" he asked.

"The Early Early Show. Look, Angie: do you know what I came over here for?"

He'd known, of course, that it couldn't be a friendly visit. "Money?"

"How did you guess?"

"I don't have any," he said. "If I did—you know."

"Let's put our heads together and see if we can't find a way to pay back his reverence, Father Phillips."

From the way she said it he knew she was angry underneath.

"He says you owe him a hundred dollars."

"Wow," Angie said.

"It seems a lot more after it's gone, doesn't it?" Julie flashed him a smile that went through him all the way to his sneakers.

He nodded.

"I feel it's my obligation as well as yours."

"No," Angie protested.

"Oh, yes. He was my guest. You've got the makings of quite a cat burglar, Angie."

"It was a kind of dare to myself. I couldn't do it again if I tried."

She looked at him, up and down. "I wouldn't recommend it myself . . . Do you know what Father Phillips is doing now?"

Angie shook his head.

"He's preaching a mission for the rest of his vacation. Salvation. I don't feel the need to be saved, do you?"

"Yes," Angie said.

She laughed aloud.

"I was thinking," Angie said a minute or two later, "maybe I could get some of the money back. Only I don't know how much I gave away. I guess it isn't such a good idea anyway. They'd've spent it."

"People you know?"

"Sort of. I mean I know one of the persons. She helped me get the money for the plane ticket."

"How much?"

"One hundred and forty-nine dollars."

"Which means you put forty-nine dollars into the suitcase."

"Fifty-seven. I had eight dollars of my own to start with. I put that in too."

"My God, what a conscience you've got."

"It was a mistake, only I didn't want to go back afterwards." He didn't want her getting any exaggerated ideas about him. He wasn't going to let anybody think what a nice boy he was anymore.

"Have you got a pencil and paper in this supply depot?" She indicated the tent.

In the back of a notebook in which he had started to write something about the stars one night—he'd only written a couple of lines—they figured out that breakfast at seven dollars and a two-dollar tip, plus three dollars cab fare plus a fifty-cent tip, plus fifty cents for the shopping bag came to thirteen dollars.

"We could have done that in our heads," Julie said. "Seven dollars for breakfast?"

"Strawberry waffles with whipped cream and stuff."

"And that's a fancy tip."

"This girl is a waitress herself. I called her Alice, only it isn't really her name."

"Tell me about her," Julie said.

Angie could feel himself going hot to the roots of his hair. He shook his head. He didn't think he could tell her about Alice.

"Oh, dear," Julie said, "that means it's going to be even harder to ask her for the money back. Did you really give her eighty-seven dollars?"

"I gave some to another woman in the park. Her name was Mag and she lives in a mansion on Twenty-first Street and Tenth Avenue."

Julie repeated the address. "That must be some mansion."

"You mean like Grand Central Station?"

"Phony. That's a tough neighborhood. I don't think we'd better count on getting anything back from her."

"She spoke really good English."

"All the more reason: she's a con artist. What did she try to sell you?"

"Nothing. I just wanted her to leave me alone which is why I gave her the money. I think I gave Alice more than her."

"Well, let's try Alice first," Julie said and got to her feet. She brushed the dust from her backside and then twisted around to look at something which would not come off.

"It looks like it's tar," Angie said. "After it cools maybe."

"After what cools?"

Angie could not explain. He felt she was teasing him.

"Never mind," Julie said. "You mustn't take me so seriously."

Alice had said something like that.

He found it easier to walk in step with Julie than he had with Alice. She walked so straight and easy. But there was an area in which he was having trouble: the closer they got to the restaurant, the less he wanted to confront Alice.

Julie said, "Don't think about it until we get there. Just let it happen when the time comes."

"How did you know what I was thinking about?"

"The way you slowed down."

"Oh." He drew a deep breath. It seemed such a long time ago he had come along this way—almost happy with the coat—and getting over the Ordeal, not knowing what was really happening to Mr. Grossman. They hadn't spoken of Mr. Grossman, Julie and him. He realized that she must know something about it, having been at the police station: that was all about Mr. Grossman. It was like knots in a string: you could go out of your mind trying to figure out which one to untie to get at the next one.

Julie asked: "Where do you live?"

"On Elizabeth Street, only I'm not going to live there anymore. My mother and I fight all the time."

"What about?"

"I don't know. Everything it seems like. It just blows up like a bottle of bad wine."

"You never know till it happens."

"Exactly," Angie said.

"Do you know anybody your age whose life is different?"

Angie thought about Ric's: he'd take his own over that. "Some are even worse."

"Some of us do something about it," Julie said. "And some don't. That's the difference. Some don't even want to do anything."

"I do," Angie said. "I mean every time I get mad, I wind up crying and then I get madder at myself. It's how I'm supposed to be super-special because of all she's done for me."

"Crap," Julie said. "She's done it for herself."

"I'm very glad to hear you say that," Angie said, "because that's how I want it. I mean this guy that's always at the house—maybe I was jealous at first, but I don't really think so, and now she says all she wants out of him is money for me—to go in business or something. I don't want to go in business. I'd run away—my father's in California—only . . ." He shrugged.

"Only what?"

"Well, I couldn't right now, with the police asking me questions . . ."

"That's an excuse."

"I guess."

"Unless you really did have something to do with Mr. Grossman's murder."

Angie became wary: it sounded as though she had set a trap for him. He looked at her, trying to figure out if she was putting on an act to get information out of him for the cop. It would be the biggest disappointment that ever happened to him.

She said, "You have a terrible home life, and a person does not have to take that, Angie, not after they're sixteen years old. Your father walked out on her, right?"

155

He nodded.

"What she's afraid of—you'll do the same thing. Now in my case, if I hadn't split when I did, my parents would be divorced. And they should be. They just stay together to blame one another for my winding up in Little Italy."

"I'll bet they're rich," Angie said.

"How did you ever guess that?"

"You're different. You even talk different. I wish I did. I had a teacher once who talked like you. I used to try to imitate him all the time, but everybody made fun of me. They made fun of him too. Then they said I had a crush on him and . . . I don't know."

"Your friends wouldn't approve of me either. I want to blow up the Establishment, and they want it to last till they can get there."

Angie only partly understood.

"Sacco and Vanzetti," she said.

"I heard of them," Angie said.

"Actually, I don't know very much about them myself except that people like me demonstrated for them—poets and actors—and they really got screwed by the Establishment."

"I'm not sure what you mean by the Establishment."

"Big business, big politics, big religion, the people who stay on top. Have you ever heard anyone talk about blowing up Con Ed?"

"I'm for that," Angie said, "what they do to the sky."

Julie smiled and set a new pace for them. "That's what it means to be anti-Establishment, and to want to do something about it."

"How did you get to walk the way you do, if you don't mind me asking?"

"It was something I admired—and I had a lot of help in school. In the kind of school I went to, posture was a big thing. And then I saw a woman once with a vase on her head, a Greek woman. She was very beautiful and I wanted to be like her."

"A Greek?" Angie said incredulously.

The restaurant was closed. One look at the traffic explained: it was all transient. The weekend visitors to Manhattan would not choose Minnie's Place short of starvation.

"I know where she lives," Angie said, and then wished he hadn't. What if she had company? He would not let anybody else say anything against Alice, but he thought about the suit of clothes and what she'd said about them. "I don't really think . . ." He stopped, taking one look at Julie: her chin was thrust out and her eyes said they were going on. He led the way across Houston Street.

There was no Alice to be expected on the mailboxes in the first-floor vestibule, but he had to look there for a clue to her real name. B for basement where G. Abramovitch lived. He repeated the name by syllables. "I guess I'd better stick to Alice if that's her."

Outdoors, Julie said, "I'll wait for you here on the steps. That would be better, don't you think? Moral support only?"

Angie nodded and went to the door beneath the steps. Alice opened it before he could ring the bell. "Lover boy!" She was wearing her duster, only it was held together with a safety pin at the important place. "I never thought I'd see you again unless it was in the newspapers."

"I'm sorry I ran out on you."

"I got the picture from the lieutenant. We got to be pretty good friends, him and me." She jerked her head toward the steps. Who's the blonde au natural?"

She'd been watching from the window, Angie realized. "She's a friend of the man I stole the sports jacket from."

"I thought she was your aunt or something. What's on your mind, Angie?"

Suddenly he was angry. "Not a thing, Miss Abraham. Not a goddam thing." He turned and took the basement steps in one stride.

"If it's the money you want back, why don't you say so?"

By then he was face to face with Julie who had heard everything. "I'll get a job someplace," he said under his breath to her.

Alice came out to the steps. "How do you do?" she said to Julie. "Angie, the lieutenant wanted to know all about your fat friend. Want to know what I told him?"

"I don't care," Angie said, but he did.

Besides, Julie had taken hold of the iron railing as though she didn't intend to move. She said, "Do you have some of the money left, Miss Abramovitch?"

Alice said, "Miss Abramovitch never spends it all in one place, honey. Come on in and bring sonny with you."

The two women got along fine. They talked about the lieutenant as though Angie wasn't present. Julie wanted to know if he was on the make and Alice wanted to know what man wasn't. Julie accepted some of the port wine that turned Angie's stomach.

"I just love it," Alice said. "Can women get gout?"

"But not from port wine," Julie said. "That's an old wives' tale."

"Those old wives could sure make them up, couldn't they?"

"It was something to do besides screwing," Julie said.

Angie could have gone through the floor. Alice laughed and said she'd get some crackers and cheese to go with the wine, and passing behind Angie, she ran her fingers through his hair. When he looked round she was winking at Julie.

He felt he was getting smaller and smaller. He imagined himself swinging his legs the way he did as a child. Then he imagined himself disappearing altogether. Where's Angie? They might not even notice he was gone. "Alice, what did the cop ask you about Ric?"

"What he looked like. How he acted."

Angie thought about it. "He knows what Ric looks like."

"That particular night. He was very interested when I said he was like a Santa Claus you pushed down and it comes back up."

That was the story of Ric's life. Maybe of his own, Angie thought.

"The lieutenant and I figured out he might've been wearing

158

something else under that sloppy sweater, like a butcher's coat stuck into his pants."

Angie remembered mostly the way Ric smelled. It made him sick thinking about it. He wished he hadn't asked Alice anything.

"I thought I ought to tell you, Angie, the lieutenant thinks maybe you were in on it with him. And stealing the coat, then coming with me the way you did gives you an alibi."

"I got the same impression," Julie said.

"I don't need an alibi," Angie said.

Alice said, "Baby, the kind of sweet shnook you are, you need an alibi even when you're innocent."

Alice and Julie got talking again, this time about Mr. Grossman and some of the things he had said to Julie about Europe before Hitler. Alice told about her relatives who had been killed in the gas ovens. Angie kept trying to get the picture and it made him want to laugh only he knew there wasn't anything funny about it. It was just that people were too big for ovens . . . Six million, Alice said, which was almost the population of New York. Angie thought of Con Ed.

Then Alice said, "I got fifty dollars for you, Angie. When I get stood up, all I want is transportation money to my next engagement."

"You do know interesting people," Julie said when she and Angie were on the street again, Angie with the fifty dollars in his pocket. "That's why I came to live in Little Italy, to meet real people. Like Alice."

"It's funny," Angie said, "I like people who aren't real better. I mean I like them the way they are in my mind."

"You mean you liked me better before you met me," Julie said.

"I didn't mean that," Angie said, but it was true. "I don't know, things really happen when I dream them."

"What I've discovered: you can dream up, but not down. What about your other friend, Mag?"

159

"It wouldn't help even if we found her. "She'd've spent the twenty bucks on bird seed by now."

"That's a lot of bird seed, but I think you're right."

"I'd buy you lunch if this money was mine," Angie said.

"We'll have lunch at my place. My credit's good at Allioto's, and I've got a check coming for *Grand Street.*"

"What did you mean, you can dream up but not down?"

"Well, you dream of being rich and successful, right?"

"I guess."

"And I want to be poor and a failure. I mean I just want to be what I turn out to be, not something coming out of the dream machine."

"Like out of television or the movies?"

"Right."

"I wouldn't mind being poor so much," Angie said thoughtfully, "if I could be successful at something that counts, a musician or a scientist . . ." He couldn't bring himself to mention dancing, not after the scene with his mother.

"Scientists are part of the Establishment. Music is too in this country. Oh, Angie, you're right. Dreaming is better."

He walked in silence for a few minutes, remembering some of his daydreams and where *doing something*—like joining the Little Brothers—had got him. Inevitably, he thought of Ric. If you were going to dream poor, his house was typical, broken down chairs they never fixed . . . "Do you ever dream of cockroaches?"

"I don't think I ever have, but there's a wonderful story—it's about a man who woke up and found himself turned into a cockroach—or maybe it's a beetle. His family doesn't recognize him, of course, and he gets an apple core lodge in the crust of his back. I'll loan it to you if you want to read it. Do you return books?"

Angie felt himself blushing.

Julie looked at him and laughed. "I'm sure you return books."

160

22 They played golf the way Marks liked to play it, with caddies and cushioned greens, honeydew melon and cheese served beneath an umbrella after the ninth hole, iced beer from a golf cart on the fifteenth tee. They were guests of a client of Julian Marks.

It was late afternoon when they got back to the clubhouse. Marks had begun to feel uneasy, out of touch. He tried to tell himself that he was only one cop on a team, a cop in a plaid shirt in East Orange. That was what was troubling him: not that he was out of touch, but that he was out of his element. He had split with the environment in which he had grown up. Not deliberately, as was the case with Julie Borghese—he realized he had been maneuvering her around this setting all afternoon—but by default. He liked to go home now and then to visit. He had the feeling that if Julie ever went home it would be to stay. Which was better, drift or drama? If Grossman had been allowed to drift in his German days, he would have stayed a musician with, say, a string quartet. Or would he have been in the pit of a theater? In a beergarden? Who would ever know? Or care. There had been cases on which he had worked where afterwards he had visited the families and sought to learn the roots of the crime . . . and to alleviate the sorrow if not the shame. Not lately. There was not much he could do about anger, and it was the principal residue on the present scene.

He got the car himself and brought it around to the clubhouse entrance where he waited for his father to exchange amenities with their host. He studied the road map and then asked someone the best way to get to Jersey City. He wasn't even sure you could get there from East Orange. One thing sure, Marks decided, it would be easier than getting from Jersey City to East Orange.

The Jersey City law offices of Galli and Frascotti were over a Liggetts drugstore. In the vestibule, Marks went through the roster. John Bonelli was a member of the firm. The offices were closed for the weekend.

Marks went into the drugstore phone booth and dialed the unlisted number. A woman answered. Marks could hear music in the background. Marks said, "Let me speak to Johnny Bonelli."

"Who's calling, please?"

"Tell him a friend of Al Ruggio's."

"Just a minute."

And very shortly, a man's voice: "Hello?"

"Johnny?"

"Yeah . . ."

Marks hung up.

23 Angie had never been in an apartment like Julie's. He had memorized everything because he felt he would be furnishing his dreams for a long time from that afternoon. Julie had put the leaves of plants under the microscope for him, and a slide with a tiny insect in a drop of water. Under the microscope it looked like a balloon with whiskers that wiggled. He had looked at the art books, and he had puzzled a great deal over the blue-robed Madonna with the words, Women's Lib, underneath. He knew what Women's Lib meant and if Julie was an example, he was for it. It was not a popular movement in Little Italy. He had been taught that the Blessed Virgin raised the dignity of women. So the two things did go together.

"Are you religious, Angie?"

"Sort of. I don't go to church much."

"Do you pray?"

"Sure. When I'm scared or want something badly enough."

"If you were to pray for something right now, what would it be?"

"Something serious?"

"The most serious."

"I'd pray they'd find whoever it was killed Mr. Grossman and it wouldn't be anybody I know."

"Angie, how did you get mixed up in that scene?"

"I can't tell you."

"Okay, but if you ever need a friend and want to, I'm here."

He had told her about his mother and Mr. Rotelli, and his

father and the brother who had left home as soon as the marines would accept him.

All this occurred during the afternoon. Toward six they walked the few blocks down Mulberry Street to the parish house and asked to see Father Phillips. They were put to wait in a small, dust-proof room where the faded chairs were covered with antimacassars.

Julie said, "I should be wearing brocade, a corset with stays, and an uplift bra."

"Yeah," Angie said, understanding in part. He also knew, having observed her carefully, that she wasn't wearing anything under the blouse.

The priest came in his shirt sleeves, wearing no collar.

"This is Angie, Father. We have some money for you."

"The acrobat," the priest said with a funny smile. "Sit down, please."

He was not like Angie had expected him to be. He tried to open the window. It wouldn't budge.

Julie said, "It doesn't open as easily as mine, Father."

Angie wished she would stop sounding so sarcastic. He handed the money to the priest in the envelope Julie had given him. "It's only fifty dollars, Father. I'll get the rest as soon as I can."

"You can send it to me," Phillips said, and buttoned the envelope into his back pants pocket. "I'll give you the address."

"In California?"

He nodded.

Julie said: "I thought you were going to preach a crusade for us."

"I've decided to practice, not preach," he said quietly.

"I was hoping you'd take my friend, Angie, to California with you. His father is there."

Angie, surprised, said: "But I don't want to go now."

"On account of me?" Julie said.

"Yes."

164

"Oh, Angie," and she put her hand on his for a moment. "You wouldn't like me for very long. I'm really not a very nice person underneath. I'm a survivor, and survivors eat the innocents first."

The priest looked at Julie for a long minute and then at Angie with that little smile again. "Do you believe her?"

"No, Father."

"Nor do I, and I don't honestly think she does either. Shall we take a little walk, the three of us, out where we can breathe?"

They went outdoors and walked down through Chinatown to the small park named after Columbus. Angie wondered what had happened to the Chinese boy at the stationhouse, but he didn't feel like trying to talk about it. He knew there was a nightmare waiting for him, but this was like a daydream and he wanted to hold onto it for as long as he could. The priest bought them Italian ices from a street vendor out of the money Angie had returned to him. There was something sad about it all. Even Julie didn't talk. They walked back in silence. The priest wrote his address on the envelope and gave it to Angie. Then he shook hands with both of them and went into the church.

Outside Julie's, Angie proposed to go up to his hideout, and he knew there was something he had to do at home.

Julie said, "If you want a meal later, just ring the bell."

When he crossed the street, by the habit of a scavenger he glanced into the uncovered trash cans at the curb. There was the cover to his *Portnoy's Complaint*, just the cover which he recognized because of the way the corners were broken off. He called out to Julie and ran back to her without even climbing the stairs to look: he knew the door to the roof would be banned to him and his gear confiscated. It upset him and he did not know why: it was not the value of the tent or supplies.

"You've been violated, your privacy invaded," Julie said when she had calmed him down.

"Maybe."

"Do you think it was the police?"

"Maybe," he said again. He was thinking of the knife he had taken away, but which remained in his father's shoe.

"Are you frightened?"

"Yeah, I guess I am, only it's different than it was before."

"Want to come upstairs?"

"I can't. There's something I've got to do."

"I understand. I don't understand, but I do. As I said before—I'll be here."

24 Julian Marks was carving the roast when Matty brought him word that there was a phone call for the lieutenant. She always took the message to him, no matter whom the call was for.

His father said, "Pour the wine first, David. Because a man has a dime in his pocket, it doesn't give him unlimited right to invade our privacy."

Marks reached for the bottle, responding by an old reflex, picked it up, and then put it down again after pouring a few drops in his father's glass. He went to the phone.

"I thought I'd better check out with you whether you'd want to take this one or not," the headquarters man said. "A Doctor Noble at Bellevue Hospital wants to talk to you. Want the number?"

"Let's have it."

While Marks waited for the hospital intercom system to track down Dr. Noble, he mused on the lives of residents and interns: no benevolent association watchdogs for them. A twenty-four-hour day came natural.

"Lieutenant? Bonelli's still here. He was discharged before noon. He started to complain about head pains, now it's stomach pains. I think he's faking. The only change in his chart is a jump in his blood pressure. I think he's scared. The preacher—the guy with the prayerbook?"

"Yes," Marks said.

"He says all these pains set in when Bonelli got a letter by messenger this morning."

"I'll come by in an hour or so," Marks said. "Thank you, doctor."

He returned to the table and noted that the wine was poured and the main course served. If either of his parents was annoyed, there was no sign. He murmured regrets.

"David," his mother said as he picked up his knife and fork, "how did your arms get to be so long?"

He was wearing his college blazer, the only jacket he had left in his parents' house. "It's not that they're longer. It's that I've filled out in the shoulders and biceps. If I had to scratch my head right now, I'd have to use my toes."

"Not at the table, David."

He and his father looked at one another.

The elder Marks said: "Mothers never allow their sons to grow up, which is virtually the only consolation left to a father after his son's bar mitzvah."

Marks stopped at his own apartment long enough to change clothes and pick up his service revolver. At the hospital, Doctor Noble had about two minutes to spare him. "Saturday night's the lonesomest night in the week. Oh, yeah? Not by Bellevue. We need the bed from under Bonelli. Try and get him to move out, will you, lieutenant? I don't know what you do in a case like this—get an eviction notice?"

Marks went to the ward by himself.

The "preacher" saluted him with two fingers, a kind of benediction as he lifted them from the prayerbook. His lips never ceased their motion. Two of the men were watching a portable television set between their beds. Bonelli lay with his eyes closed, his fingers working a little where his hands were folded on his stomach. The dark splotches under his eyes were beginning to green.

"Bonelli."

He jumped, opening his eyes. "Who let you in?"

"I have visiting privileges," Marks said.

"I asked so nobody comes to see me. I'm sick. I think I'm bleeding inside."

"In your case, that's better than bleeding on the outside. Who are you afraid of, Bonelli?"

"You. You want the God's truth, you."

Marks sat down at the bottom of the bed.

"Get up," Bonelli said. "You're making me sicker."

"You mean a visit from a detective working on the Grossman case got you into trouble. Isn't that it?"

"I don't know what you're talking about."

"Did Ric come to see you today?"

"No. I thought I was going home till I got this attack."

"Gall bladder?" Marks suggested.

"Tell the doctor that, will you? It could be gall bladder. Down somewhere inside."

"Who was the letter from this morning?"

"My son the lawyer. He wants me to get well."

The preacher, whose ears were as keen as his eyes, said, "Policeman, you know what he did with the letter?"

"Shut your mouth. When I get up, I break your foot."

"You break my foot, I break your ass." The preacher crossed his lips with his thumbnail. "He put it down the toilet."

Marks pretended to ignore the information. "So you didn't know Grossman. How about the man named Ruggio in the upstairs apartment? He's been missing for thirty-six hours."

"Never heard of him!"

"He's a friend of Johnny's."

"That's a lie!"

"I thought you never heard of him."

"I don't. I know Johnny got no friends in Little Italy I don't know about. My son is a good man, Mr. Detective. Don't you hurt my son."

For the older one he would die, Marks thought. The younger one was something else. "I don't intend to hurt him. All I want to know right now is what's hurting you so much."

"My gall bladder."

"Where's Johnny's office?"

"I only know in New Jersey. He works for somebody else."

"In Jersey City. He's in the firm of Galli and Frascotti."

"Why do you ask me questions when you know?"

"To find out how well you know your own son."

"I know him!" he cried and pounded on his chest.

"Did he warn you to stay in the hospital for your own safety, Bonelli?"

"You crazy cop! Get out of here. I'm a sick man."

Marks got up. "You know, I'm probably the only person in this hospital who believes it? I'm going to ask them to keep you for another twenty-four hours."

Marks felt a small prickle of elation as he got his car out of the hospital parking lot. He was also aware of his first personal fear during the investigation. He proposed to go no further than headquarters without a partner, and as he drove those few blocks he kept a tight vigil in the rear-view mirror.

When he walked into the squadroom, there was Tomasino, turning the pages of the file. He was still in formal dress, but with his black tie badly askew.

"It must have been quite a wedding," Marks said.

"It was, only I couldn't get with it, you know?"

"I know," Marks said, and gave him an affectionate poke in the arm. "Anything new?" He pointed to the file.

"She went out as far as the delicatessen for milk and bread. Took the baby with her. She's back in."

"Find yourself some work clothes. I'm going to put the all points out on Ruggio. Then we've got a job to do."

"What?"

"Take the fat boy apart, even if we can't put him together again."

Tomasino spat on his hands. "It'll be a pleasure."

Everybody's punching bag, as the old lady said. Humpty Dumpty. Marks did not relish the job, but it had to be done.

When Ric opened the door to the two detectives, his first words were, "What's happened to Pa?"

He almost had to have been expecting them, Marks thought. Was his concern for his father genuine, or a cover for his own fear? "That's why we're here. What did happen to him?"

"I mean he's all right, isn't he?"

"Scared half to death, but that shouldn't surprise you."

The fat one sucked in his breath. "I thought he was dead or something."

"From what causes, Ric?"

"Him not coming home," the boy said. He wore a clean white shirt—dressed up even to the point of cuff-links and polished shoes.

"Let's go over what happened out here first," Marks said. "Show me where he was standing when you hit him with the bottle."

"I didn't. I broke the bottle just to scare him. The railing there broke when he backed into it. The wood's rotten. The whole building's rotten."

"Why the big routine at the Little Brothers then?" Marks led the way into the apartment. Ric did not try to stop them. The first thing the detective noticed was a cracked bowl on the table with fruit in it, a couple of apples and some expensive oranges.

"I'm always complaining about how Pa treats me. Like some big cry-baby. The Brothers don't have any respect for me. So I made it up."

"I see," Marks said. He reached for one of the oranges and looked to catch the boy's reaction.

Ric didn't want him to have it, but he smirked and murmured, "Pa likes oranges."

Marks put it back in the bowl, trying not to feel sorry for this lump of blubber. The broken window had been replaced with cardboard, probably the laundry backing for the shirt Ric now wore. The place was filthy underneath. Marks could smell it, but on the surface it wasn't bad: he'd worked hard, trying to clean it.

"Sit down," Marks said, and when the boy had seated himself on a chair the springs of which dragged the floor, "Tommy, close the door." He took a large plastic bag from his pocket, shook it out so that Ric could see its size. He put it over the back of a chair. "Before we go, I want the clothes you were wearing Thursday night—the black sweater, pants, whatever you were wearing underneath, and your shoes."

"They ain't here," Ric said. He moistened his lips. "They're at the plant."

"We'll drive you over and get them. I understand there's a watchman. He'll let us in."

"I'll lose my job. You can have the shoes. I'm wearing them now."

"And your underwear?"

"I don't wear any. I'll get the pants for you . . ." Ric started to get up.

"No hurry," Marks said. He could give them any old pair hanging in the closet, Marks knew. It was the sweater he wanted and either that was clean, in his terms, or they weren't going to get it. A psychological advantage was the best he could hope for. "Let's go over your timetable for Thursday night." Marks took pen and notebook from his pocket. "The argument between you and your father was going strong by eleven o'clock, according to one witness. Right?"

"I don't know. Me waking up all of a sudden. She always exaggerates anyway." He jerked his head toward the Niccoli apartment.

"You smashed the window and then it was quiet for some time. Where did you go for the wine?"

"Mike's place."

"Was that before or after you went to Grossman's?" Marks asked without a change of inflection.

The boy's ruddy face went pale in blotches. Again he wet his lips. "I want to call my brother. He's a lawyer."

Marks motioned toward the phone. It was on the same table as the fruit. Ric shook his head. He looked from Marks to Tomasino and back at Marks again.

"Call him," Marks said.

"I guess not."

"Why not, Ric? It's your right."

"He wouldn't do anything for me. I don't know. I don't even know where to call him."

"I'll give you the number."

"No."

"Ric, what were you doing outside of Grossman's at eleven-thirty Thursday night?"

"I was looking for Angie."

Tomasino scribbled his shorthand: it was their first real break. The scratch of his pen drew Ric's attention.

Marks said, "Were you supposed to meet him there?"

"No. It was just . . ." He shrugged.

"Why were you looking for him?"

"Somebody I could talk to," Ric said. "I was going to tell him about me and Pa, you know, the way I said at the club?"

"About hitting him over the head with the bottle?"

"Yeah."

"But that didn't happen until twelve-thirty."

"You mixed me up. I was looking for Angie."

"But why there, Ric? Doesn't Angie live *down* the street from here?"

"He wasn't home."

"Did you go to his house?"

"No. I just knew he wasn't home."

"Where was he?"

"He's got a hideout someplace. I was looking for him. That's all."

"A man named Ruggio—do you know him?"

"Never heard of him."

"A friend of your brother Johnny's."

"Huh?" That surprised him, Marks realized. It was new information to the boy and he didn't know what to do with it in his own mind. Marks had a hunch that it pleased him.

"Come on, Ric. You're going to tell us sooner or later. When you and your father quarreled about money, where did Grossman come in on it?"

Ric wiped the sweat from his face with his hand and his hand on the filthy upholstery. "I always thought Pa was going to him for money. Borrowing, I mean, and I was going to have to pay it back."

"You always thought . . . When did you find out he wasn't?"

"He told me."

"He told you he was peddling dope for Grossman."

"He wasn't," Ric said, and repeated the words several times, half-crying.

Marks tried another tack: "The Little Brothers were going to save him. Is that it?"

Ric sniffed and nodded.

"By killing Grossman?"

"Not by killing him."

"By what then? Some hocus-pocus?" Marks thought of the swastikas and the clean square of window. "Am I right, Tommy? A secret society—some kind of curse was put on the man."

Tomasino said, "Ric, the Little Brothers or your father, who are you going to protect?"

"Pa."

"Then what did the Little Brothers do to Grossman?"

Ric told of the ritual, of Angie's having to put the Killing Eye on Grossman.

"How did you know he was pushing drugs?" Tomasino asked.

"Angie got the proof, a black man, and him paying off the cops. I mean we all figured it out first which is why Angie got the Ordeal."

"The Ordeal," Marks repeated. He thought he was close now: the Blacks moving in on the Family. Bonelli's money coming to an end: it coincided with Ruggio's moving into the apartment on Hester Street. The crippled Bonelli was all right as a go-between between the Syndicate and Grossman, and Family benevolence required that he be taken care of. But when the Black takeover became a possibility, they needed a Ruggio.

But why take out Grossman?

"When you got to Grossman's that night, did you see Angie?"

"No, sir."

It was the first *sir* he had gotten throughout the interrogation.

"And what did you do?"

"I hung around and I saw a girl going into Grossman's. I thought it was for stuff and Angie not even seeing her when he was supposed to be there. I was going to bring him up before the Little Brothers. You know, I was going to take over the Eye till midnight like he was supposed to, but I seen a man watching me so I beat it for home, and I got the old man his fucking wine on the way."

Marks thought of Angie on the backless chair. "Did you accuse Angie?"

"That's what I was going to do when you guys showed up. When you went out, Louis disbanded us till things cooled."

Marks did not think Ric could put it together that well if it was not the truth. When he glanced questioningly at Tomasino, the younger detective nodded. He was willing to buy it.

Ric's white shirt was wilted, the boy soaked with sweat. He complained of how he was trying to look decent in case his father came home.

"Take another bath," Tomasino said. "It won't hurt you."

Marks left the plastic bag on the chair. "Bring us the sweater, Ric."

Mrs. Niccoli directed them from her sidewalk chair to where Angie Palermo lived, and this without their even asking. "She *is* a witch," Marks said.

They rang the vestibule bell which might or might not work and then went up to the third-floor apartment and at the door there rang the buzzer several times. No one came. Then, from the floor below, a woman called: "Who's up there?"

Marks looked down at the heavy-set woman. "We're looking for Angie Palermo."

"I'm looking for him too. I'm his mother."

The detectives went down and exchanged a few words with her. She had been a handsome woman once, but she had let herself go and she was bitter. "Everybody says what a good boy he is, like I've been telling my neighbor . . ."

The neighbor nodded from the doorway.

Marks thanked them.

"When you find him," Mrs. Palermo called after the detectives, "tell him if he don't come home tonight, he don't ever need to come home. He can go to his father . . . He can go to hell." Before they reached the street, she was running after them. "I don't mean that. I'm worried out of my mind. Tell him . . . please, to come home."

The detectives went next to Angie's hideout, and found the roof hatch padlocked.

"It's a fire trap," Tomasino said. It seemed to outrage him. He put the ladder to the frame, went up it, and with several thrusts of his shoulder, opened the door. He had torn the hasp from the wood.

They went onto the roof and found Angie's things gone. Across the way, Julie's lights were on, her shades up. She was sitting near the fan, a book in her hand.

"I thought he'd come back," Julie said. "In fact, I thought it might be him now."

"Where to look next," Marks said. "Any clues, Julie?"

"I thought he'd come here, I mean in preference to going home. But I shouldn't judge by what I'd do."

You'll go home soon, Marks thought, but he didn't say it.

"Is he in danger—I mean his life or something like that?"

"Something like that. It depends on what he saw at Grossman's. Or who he saw at Grossman's."

"It's heroin isn't it?"

"Did Angie tell you that?"

"Angie told me about nothing, Lieutenant Marks, except his home life and himself personally."

"Then how did you know it was heroin?"

"I guessed it. A person with an idea of what's going on in the world would—including the local police whom you're supposed to support—and everybody around here does."

"You couldn't bring yourself to tell us that, could you, Miss Julie?"

"I don't support my local police."

"You'd better, young lady. Some day you may need them." Marks signaled Tomasino: they were leaving.

Julie said, "Try Father Phillips."

"We will."

"And if he does come back, I'll keep him here and let you know."

"Thank you," Marks said. Nevertheless, his enchantment, such as there had been of it, was ended.

Phillips had not seen the boy since Julie and he had come to him that afternoon. At the rectory door, the priest said, "If it's any use to you, I think I could say almost positively the fat boy in the lineup this morning was the person I saw while waiting for Miss Borghese."

Marks could not conceal his disgust. "What was it, Father? Didn't you want to get involved?"

"I don't think it was that—but I may have been deceiving myself."

"He has already identified himself," Marks said. What he did not say was that it came about because Marks had used Phillips' reluctant testimony anyway.

On the way uptown they stopped at Hester Street. The stakeout car was empty.

The Ruggio apartment was in darkness, and the police seal had been removed from the door to Grossman's shop.

Tomasino went back to the car to make radio contact with headquarters. Marks went into the delicatessen.

"It happened mighty fast," Allioto said, "her and the baby getting into the car, and one of the men throwing a little suitcase in after her."

"Did you see the license plate on the car?"

"It was a police plate. The guy with the suitcase was one of your own men."

"I wonder what language they communicated in," Marks said, almost to himself. He had a premonition of total failure.

"Huh?" Allioto said.

"She couldn't speak English, that's all I'm saying." Marks was on his way.

"Hey, lieutenant," Allioto called after him.

Marks paused at the door.

"She could speak English. She couldn't speak Italian, but she could speak English."

"Oh, my God," Marks said after a few seconds of thought.

Tomasino brought the car to a screaming halt at the door. Marks got in. Tomasino said, "We're to drop it, Dave. There's orders from the top to come in without delay."

"Then let's ride."

"What does it mean?"

"I think we've come damn near blowing the cover on a Narcotics agent. Ruggio was probably a Federal plant."

There was neither confirmation nor denial of this information waiting for them when they reached the division offices, only the cold order from Inspector Fitzgerald to suspend further investigation of Grossman's death until instructed to proceed.

Marks and Tomasino sat, trying to put the pieces together to their own satisfaction; this in the midst of other men responding to other violence in their part of the city.

"Oh, man," Tomasino said. "It's like trying to find the bathroom in the dark."

"When you don't know where it is," Marks added. Which took him back in his mind's eye to the lone commode in the three-story building, near which Grossman had been murdered. "Ruggio would have found the body when he came in that night, late. One A.M. or so. He had to choose between reporting to us or to the mob who thought he was their man. He called Johnny Bonelli and got their orders: find the body in the morning. Then he showed up on the loading dock . . . and I don't know where Ruggio goes from there."

"What about Bonelli, the lawyer—which side is he on?"

Marks thought of the father in the hospital and his fierce pride in his older son, and he thought of Gerosa's story of his struggle as a young lawyer to stay clean of Family. "I've got a hunch he's Ruggio's partner—undercover."

"Family inside family," Tomasino said. "I'm going home to mine, Dave, and glad of it."

A window within a window, Marks thought. Which association brought him back to Angie.

25 If Angie had not been on the lookout for Ric, the detectives would have caught him, and with the knife in his belt. If she had wanted to, old Mrs. Niccoli could have told them that he was home. On his way home from Julie's he had waved at her when she called out to him that Ric was looking for him. He had heard his mother's voice in the apartment beneath theirs, and he had prayed with all his might that he could get into the house and out of it again, with the knife, without his mother's hearing him. His footstep was softer than his heartbeat. But before leaving he had looked out to see if Ric was on the street, and he had seen Marks and Tomasino. He hid himself in his own closet and waited, unable to plan beyond the moment.

But they went away and his mother did not come. He was not sure, on the street, whether Mrs. Niccoli had seen him leave or not, but he went the long way around, and on Mott Street decided to go one more block to Mulberry in case Ric had gotten wise to the route by which Angie avoided him. He stepped into a doorway or ducked down between parked cars whenever a vehicle passed. He imagined Marks cruising the area looking for him.

He did not know why the knife had become such a terror to him: he was afraid to have it and afraid not to have it. It didn't have to do with the murder. Even if Ric told the police he had it . . . and he was sure Ric would if he got the chance. Whenever Ric said he wasn't going to tell, it meant he was going to. The knife was part of Angie's innocence, and yet he was afraid of it. It was also part of his strength, and that was what he was afraid of. That was why he had to put it somewhere where he could never find it again. He'd told his mother he had thrown it in the river, and that was where it belonged. He reached Canal Street and felt a little safer. But from what? As soon as he crossed the Bowery, and he had to do so, he would be in foreign territory. He found himself rubbing the sheath like the knife was a charm or even something alive he was taking care of . . . like a part of himself that was vulnerable. He started to run before he reached Elizabeth, just in case, and then wondered why he had come so close to home again when he'd wanted to go toward the East River all the time. It was the way he knew, that was all. He thought of going to Julie's and asking her to come with him. He decided that he would go back to Julie's when it was over. It was something to look forward to.

"Hey, Angie. Wait up."

Running toward him on Elizabeth Street—so that they would have almost collided if Angie hadn't started to run when he did—came Ric.

Angie might have outrun him, but with the bridge traffic and the traffic lights on the Bowery, Ric might have caught up. Angie waited. It wasn't a bad idea to have Ric with him. Since Ric knew he had the knife, why not let him see it disappear into the river?

They did not speak at first, walking side by side, Ric panting for breath. Ric had on a white shirt and cuff-links that sparkled whenever they caught the light.

"Where are you going this way?"

"To the river." He intended to give no advance information.

They crossed the Bowery, dodging men who could hold their hands out but couldn't keep their heads up.

"I don't like it over here," Ric said.

Angie didn't answer him. They went down alongside the bridge where the arches rose like the inside of a church. Construction cranes were parked where the street was blocked off. There were sewage pipes you could almost walk through. Red warning lanterns blinked where rocks were piled. Abandoned cars scattered the street. People sneaked among them.

"It's spooky," Ric said. "Tell me where you're going." He grabbed at Angie's arm.

"Keep your dirty hands off me!" Angie said it. He'd always wanted to and always wound up saying it to himself only. He knew it was because of the knife that he was brave. What was he going to do when he lost it? Start hiding again?

"Don't give me that," Ric said, but he put his hands in his pockets and trudged along in silence.

Angie kicked a beer can out of his way. It ricocheted among cement blocks and sent up a clattering echo into the hum of overhead traffic.

"What are you sore at?"

"A lot of things," Angie said.

"The cops know about the Killing Eye," Ric said. "Did you tell them?"

"No."

"Somebody did."

Which meant, Angie thought, that Ric had told them. "I don't care."

"You better. They're looking for you."

"Let 'em."

"Let's go home. Come on, Angie." But he didn't touch him.

"No." He wanted to turn back himself, but he wasn't going to, not until he'd done what he had to do. He had said No to his mother, too, and then he had lied, but it was not because he was afraid of her.

"Pa ain't come home and he was supposed to."

Angie tried to think how he could get rid of Ric afterwards so that he could go to Julie's.

"They could kill him," Ric said.

"Who?"

"Angie, you know the guy, Ruggio, the cops think killed Grossman?"

"Yes."

"Let's sit down some place. I can't talk and walk at the same time."

"Not till we get to the river," Angie said.

"But there'll be people there."

"So what?"

"You got the knife with you, don't you?"

"So what?" Angie said again.

"Let me see it, Angie."

"In the gut if you touch me!"

Ric gave him a shove.

"Cut it out, Ric."

"Don't smart-ass me then. I'm trying to tell you something."

"I don't want to know!"

"That ain't going to help anything, not knowing!" and the words began to burst out of Ric like the flood from an open hydrant. "Years and years, Pa was pretending he didn't know, going from the Jew to somebody in the Family, carrying them money, nigger money, dope money, blood money, do you know what I'm saying? They made him do it after he got hurt because he wanted to put my fucking brother through law school. And what happens? All of a sudden the Jew don't want him anymore, and they put this guy Ruggio in Pa's job. And Pa starts crying to me about the Jew, what he did to him. And you know what? The big-shot lawyer, my fucking brother Pa was always comparing me to, you know what? He's in the Family. He's Mafia, Angie. I could die laughing if it wasn't for Pa. Let's sit down. I'm going to be sick if we don't. The rotten cops took all the sweat out of me. My mouth's like it's full of cotton."

So they sat down on a pile of cement blocks, and Angie thought he had been right: Ric had told the cops about the Killing Eye. He tried to think about what Ric had just said and what it meant to him, Angie, when the detective started going over him again.

He could hear Ric's heavy breathing with a wheeze at the end of each breath. A gang of kids bore down on one of the abandoned cars they had passed, bits of their talk coming through in waves, then fading out. Spanish. They were on Puerto Rican ground.

"Let me see the knife, Angie. I won't take it. I swear. Little Brother's oath."

After he'd told about the Killing Eye.

But Angie took the knife from its sheath. He held it fast,

looping his index and forefinger round the hilt. The blade shone in the semi-darkness. He couldn't tell if Ric was looking at it, his face in shadow.

"I wish I was dead. You'd do me a favor," Ric said.

Angie stuck the knife away and started to get up. Ric pulled him down.

"I killed Grossman and I don't even know what for."

"Tell it to the cops!" Angie screamed. He wrenched free of Ric's grip and started to run, but Ric tripped him and he fell headlong. Ric threw himself on top of Angie. Angie could turn only his head, and his mouth was full of dirt. "Goddamn you, Ric."

"You're going to listen to me, Angie. Somebody's going to listen to me, and you're going to believe me."

Angie couldn't feel the knife where it ought to have been. He'd lost it, falling. He squirmed and writhed, but he could not get out from under Ric who now sat astride him and pinned his shoulders to the ground.

"You think I'm lying, but I'm not. I got the knife at home I stole from the plant a long time ago, and when Pa started on me that night—like he said I was a fat carcass you couldn't tell from a hanging cow, I wanted to kill him. I got the knife and chased him with it. He banged the window out and started yelling for help. I had to get out of the house or I would have killed him . . ."

Ric bent over him to where he was sobbing in Angie's ear and slobbering on his cheek. Angie turned his face the other way but Ric was there too. "I went looking for you like I always do, and when I got to Grossman's and didn't see you, I figured you could've been hiding up in the hall or in the can, waiting to scare him. I went up and looked. I even said, Angie, under my breath, on account of Ruggio upstairs. I was crazy, thinking of Pa. I never did nothing to him. I can't help being like me . . ."

Angie tried not to hear. He kept pumping his backside, trying to throw Ric off. Then he lay still because it hurt.

"When the Jew came upstairs, I was by the window that's

boarded up. He couldn't see me. He wasn't even looking, and when he bent over to unlock the door—it was so easy, Angie. I just dug the knife in his back and kept doing it till he went down. When I got home and told Pa, he said, You crazy bastard, I should've drowned you when you were born. *Why didn't he?*" Ric pounded his fists into Angie's back.

"Don't, Ric. Please . . ."

Ric stopped. "Say you believe me."

"I believe you."

Ric tumbled off him and rolled over on his back. Angie got to his knees. The white shirt made Ric look like half a person.

Angie did not believe him. He wanted to, but he couldn't. He saw the knife, the blade partly under Ric. The handle was within Angie's reach.

Ric said: "I didn't see the fucking cat till it started growling. He was holding it in his arms when he fell down dead and let it go. It jumped at me like a tiger and I caught it on the blade of the knife. Clean through. It stuck there."

Angie believed him. He pulled his own knife from beneath Ric and held it over him. He was not afraid and he had the strength. But he also had the strength to open his hand and let the knife fall out of it. He got to his feet and with every step away his legs grew steadier until he was able to run.

He told the story first to Father Phillips, and then to Marks when the priest called him and the detective came to the rectory. The two men agreed afterwards that Angie should remain with Phillips for the time being.

He was given a small room and slept in a priest's bed. On the wall over his head was a crucifix entwined with palms. The housekeeper brought him tea and cinnamon toast, and Father Phillips sat with him for a long time talking of many things, but mostly about the priest himself, and how he had become a priest, and the school where he taught in California. Finally, well past midnight, and because he had not yet said his office of the day, Phillips brought his breviary and read it aloud. Angie fell asleep before he had finished.

26 Marks picked up Ric Bonelli when he returned home and booked him for homicide at the stationhouse just down the street from where he lived.

During the night, Federal, state, and city Narcotics agents moved on the Ruggio information. Nowhere, as the story developed in the days following and key underworld figures were indicted, was there mention of John Bonelli. Marks was going to have to wait to see if Ric involved his brother. To Marks' own belief, the older Bonelli son had performed a dangerous liaison, acting with Special Agent Ruggio. Narcotics officials would, of course, protect their sources.

The only heroin left on Grossman's premises was in the statuette of St. Francis Marks had held in his own hand in the Ruggio apartment. The shipments to Grossman as they left Italy were perfectly clean, so many statues of St. Joseph, St. Francis, Virgins . . . as invoiced. But at a port of call, generally Marseilles, a seaman returning from shore leave would bring aboard a number—in the last instance—of St. Francises, each narcotics-filled. Somewhere on the high seas, the originals went overboard.

When Marks was asked by a reporter what in his part of the investigation gave him the greatest satisfaction, he said off the top of his head, "That I never did catch up with Ruggio." Then he added: "But if you print it, you'll never make copy from me again."

Angie Palermo—16
7 Ars.   " — Mr. Rothies ...

"Fat Ric"

Tony
Pete De Fork
Gabby
Ric
Pig Louis